A Chosen Landscape

Adventures in the Gay Academy

Jon W. Finson

Copyright ©2016 Jon W. Finson

All rights reserved.

This novel is a work of fiction. Names, characters, places, and incidents are either the product of the author's imagination or are used fictitiously, and any resemblance to actual persons, living or dead, events, or locales is entirely coincidental.

All lyrics are quoted and in the public domain (my thanks to Troy Schreck at Alfred Music Publishing in confirming this status for Dion Titheradge's "And Her Mother Came Too").

All translations of foreign lyrics by the author, save for "Philenes Lied" trans. by Theodore Martin, published in Goethe, *Wilhelm Meister's Apprenticeship* (Leipzig: Bernhard Tauchnitz, 1873).

Cover photograph: public domain
.

CreateSpace Independent Publishing Platform

ISBN-10: 1522803556
ISBN-13: 978-1522803553

For all the men of my earlier years
à la recherche du temps perdu

Your soul is a chosen landscape
Where charming maskers and mummers promenade,
Playing the lute and dancing and somewhat
Sad beneath their fantastic disguises.

While all of them sing in a minor key
Of victorious love and the good life,
They lack an air of believing in their happiness,
And their song mingles with the moonlight.

With the serene moonlight, sad and lovely,
That sets the birds in the trees to dreaming
And makes the fountains sob with ecstasy,
The tall, thin fountains amid the marble statues.

—Paul Verlaine

CONTENTS

	Acknowledgments	i
1	Awakening Gay	1
2	In the Groves of Academe	13
3	A Separate Truce	24
4	Housemates with Benefits	36
5	*Ménages Étranges*	47
6	Summer Beauties`	57
7	Fall Teams	69
8	Stylists and Florists and Clerks, Oh My!	81
9	The Din of Onset	96
10	*Quem Diligit Anima Mea*	107
11	*Anschluß!*	121
12	The Most Unkindest Cut	133
13	Come to the Cabaret	152
14	Ties That Bind	171
15	Migration	187
16	*Plaudite Amici*	210

ACKNOWLEDGMENTS

With thanks to the many friends who have encouraged my writing, especially Lori, Sue, Jackie and Gary, David, Lisa, Bill, Rob, Paul, Ken, and the others who have read drafts or offered comments on my fiction. Without their support and reflection I could not have persisted in this journey.

1 AWAKENING GAY

My mother and I didn't entirely agree about two things when she finally made me come out (with a simple direct question when I turned 31). The first item concerned any role she may have played in my sexual preferences. Neither she nor my father exerted any such influence. My love of other men came as part of the original equipment, designed by the manufacturer and installed at the factory. The mechanism did not bear alteration, nor would any non-factory replacement parts do. I had known since my fourth year that men attracted me. By my sixth year, roughhousing with the neighborhood children, I knew that I liked the warm, innocent touch of the older boys on my skin.

When I reached thirteen, I finally put a name to this allure, thanks to an article in the June 26, 1964 issue of *Life* magazine under the title "Homosexuality in America," with the subheading "A secret world grows open and bolder. Society is forced to look at it—and try to understand it." Aha, *I* was a "homosexual," a member of the "gay world . . . ." It gave the line "don we now our . . ." a whole new twist. And I can't say that I viewed it as the "sad and often sordid world" *Life* described, though it would have its perils.

If I came into the world gay, I must relate, to be fair, that my mother aided significantly with awakening realization, though I never let her know (God bless her!). She loved American musical comedy, and she had a particular fondness for *South Pacific*. She considered me too young to understand its more adult themes when it first came out on film in 1958. But 20th Century Fox re-released it for a second run during the summer of—you guessed it—1964. Having turned thirteen, my mother deemed me old enough to understand the sexual undertones of the story—not as she had intended, but all too well. She dropped me off at the theater for a Saturday matinee, and the sight of half-naked Seabees singing "There Is Nothing Like a Dame" took my breath away. Even more so the entrance of a slender but well-built John Kerr, on whom I immediately formed a school-boy crush (especially with his shirt off). For many years he remained my "type," not that I'm exclusive on that point. I phoned my mother as soon as the first showing finished to ask whether I could stay for another. Thanks to *Life, South Pacific*, and my mother (Saints preserve her!), I had all the information I needed to write my own lyrics: "There Is Nothing Like a Dude" (to employ an anachronistic colloquialism).

Those of you who've been counting probably wonder whether I've forgotten about the other part of my opening promissory note. *Second*, my mother predicted that as a gay man I'd be lonely for the rest of my days. She mistook that one even more than the what-did-I-do-to-make-you-gay item. Being gay has formed the very best part of my life. It's been at turns amusing, instructive, steamy, and entirely enjoyable (even though I lived through the painful years when many friends passed away in their prime). I often think that some people resent gay men because we have so much better sex (I've tried it both ways—eat your hearts out, breeders). As I grew older, I discovered that I could walk into any gay bar, and all the men there would have shared some version of my experience. Almost all of them had to face coming out eventually: even today one must let the family know, whether they like it or not. And friends sometimes discover it early. Because just when hormones summon the cravings of lust and you're trying to fit in with the crowd, you find out that the crowd you most enjoy showers with you after gym. Eat your hearts out again, breeders: how much would you have paid in high school for a ticket to the women's locker room? The memory of gay adolescence creates an immediate bond across all cultures.

My mother should have suspected I would find this bond. For as odd as it may seem, she and my father had visited gay bars in New York while he studied law there after World War II. At one point I dared ask why they had explored outré locales, and she replied that they wanted to acquaint themselves with all aspects of life. They bestowed this gift on their child too.

"If you aren't enjoying yourself," my father once imparted a very rare piece of unsolicited advice, "Stop and do something else. Life's too short." After I came out he defended me against all challengers. When I'd return home in the wee hours after prowling around Chicago, my mother would start to object but my father would rebuke her: "Adrianna, he's a young man. Let him have some fun!" He followed this with his usual quip, "Don't marry, son, until you're 35." I could tell you now whether I lasted that long, but I don't want to run ahead of my tale.

When I attended prep school, a local private academy, as the privileged son of well-to-do parents, I followed social norms, in spite of my attraction to other boys. I dated girls and made a kind of fumbling love to them. If you ask how a fundamentally gay young man can do this, I would answer that most adolescents have an indiscriminate carnal appetite, and they will satisfy it with any available resource (when I'm not close to the one that I long for, I long for the one I'm near). Let me translate that for you into plain English (since I write and speak like the over-educated college professor I am): horny is horny—any port will do in a hormonal storm.

I experimented with boys too, of course, though nothing heavy at first. My friends taught one another how to pleasure themselves (translation: masturbate, buff the banana, pump the python, flog the log, spank the monkey, choke the chicken—add slang as appropriate and beat until stiff white peaks emerge). This started on overnights with one of the neighbor boys, and it continued for a good year and a half, until one magic night we produced liquid results. That ended two-man sessions for him, but not for me. I liked touching my male friends, and I managed to teach four or five others this terrific and entertaining pastime.

Since I went to a day school, exploratory massage with my schoolmates pretty much ended for a couple of years after we turned fourteen (I'm sorry I missed boarding school, in a way, since men I met later from that background had a lot more experience in their youth and had gone further than just using their hands). But I found another outlet soon enough. And so, in this series of portraits capturing my friends and companions, I must relate my first romance (puppy love, combined with fierce and seemingly constant arousal that should have sent me, had I known, to a doctor for "erections lasting more than four hours").

The old German folk song runs:

> Oh Mum, I'd like a something,
> Thing-a-ling ding ding,
> A thing, a thing.
> What d'you want my dearest child?
> Oh, Mother, oh! You're no darn good
> If you can't guess my deepest wish
> And heart's desire.
> Thing-a-ling ding ding,
> Thing-a-ling ding ding!

He went by the name of Wes Carey, and although he was an "older man" (I was sixteen when I encountered him first, he a worldly-wise nineteen) it would be entirely unfair and inaccurate to say that he "recruited" me. Quite the contrary—I precociously seduced him. Of course you want to hear all about that, but let me describe him first.

Wes served in the Army as a specialist assigned to a local radar installation—part of the Nike anti-aircraft system protecting the metropolitan area in those still tense days following the Cuban missile crisis. After my tale of *South Pacific*, you can imagine that I would succumb to almost any man in uniform, especially in olive drabs or khakis. And the exotic appearance of a soldier in the elite north-suburban climes of greater Chicago magnified this susceptibility. Nearby reservists flew their required hours from Glenview Navel Air Station, but they were largely married men. And had I traveled a little further north, I could have encountered the sailors at Great Lakes Navel Training Center or the men stationed at Fort Sheridan. But none of these wandered into my high-school purview. Wes, posted not half a mile away, worked in his off hours at a hardware store where I took an after-school and weekend job (my parents had profound faith in the work ethic).

Just then I thought Wes the most fetching thing I had ever seen, with his lithe, muscular body, toothsome grin, short-cut curly hair, and rural Pennsylvanian accent. To watch him arrive in the back of the store and change out of fatigues into the costume of a floor assistant was thrilling. He held the rank of corporal with a playful sense of humor, and I was a high-school student with a huge crush. He clearly liked chumming around with me, and he knew something of what we called then "best buddies." I could make him laugh; he could impress me with his store of worldly wisdom as well as a rich vocabulary of Army slang. I hatched a plot, though, to take the friendship to another level. I thought at the time that he tended toward the straight side of bisexuality. But a tall, high-school swimmer with good looks intrigued him, and all human relationships have an erotic component. Ours just became more than Platonic.

Our involvement went through stages over the course of a year, beginning with lunches and then widening into evenings out. And what evenings out: I don't think I was ever so impressed as when he took me to the non-commissioned officers club at Fort Sheridan for my seventeenth birthday (the age of consent in Illinois, which had decriminalized homosexuality in 1961). Surrounded by men in uniform, living in barracks yet! He'd order two beers for himself and then sneak one to me (nobody there ever carded me, because a lot of the soldiers looked young). He also passed me paperback novels that he had read as he whiled away the empty hours tending the radar screens at his post. And one of these books sent a message: Mary Renault's *The Last of the Wine*, the story of two Greek lovers in the time of Socrates, placed at the top of a pile of assorted literature. Now I not only had a crush on an "older man" but also a narrative to go with it. I took it as an invitation.

Radar specialists did not quarter permanently on base; Wes had to rent a room in a suburban home nearby. And so one night, after we had returned to his place from a dinner out at the non-com club, both a little buzzed, we went up to his room and started wrestling, just horseplay. Then I brushed the fly of his uniform and discovered he had a pronounced bulge. I brushed my hand over it casually a few more times and then moved in for a real massage. Wes became very quiet, offering mock resistance, "Hey Nick, what ya doin' there?" I made no reply, but he didn't retreat. After a little more kneading, I unzipped him and his beautifully up-curved erection popped right out, ready for action. I don't know whether he thought this might happen or not, but he followed the soldier's motto, "A stiff cock has no conscience." As a polite lad, he reciprocated. This first time we didn't go much further than I had with my junior-high buddies: mutual massage until we gushed, though Wes insisted we remove our clothes so as not to "mess up my uniform." Let's face it: he just liked skin on skin.

Wes would have contentedly remained at this level, but I wanted more. His menu didn't feature conventional kissing. But when I moved my lips lower down on the second night, he objected disingenuously, "Whoa, Nick, pretty wild!" I looked up right into his deep brown eyes, "I can stop." But I couldn't unring that bell or put the toothpaste back in his tube for that matter. He loved it, and, of course, he returned the favor. He never said it in so many words, but I could tell he liked the flavor of what I had to offer: clam sauce without the linguini (no limp noodles here).

We repeated this drill several times that night, just to make sure we had it right. I went as far as sticking my finger up his tight hole to make him spurt (he moaned and exploded every time, one of those men who had tremors after they climaxed—you know the type). And he practiced this drill on me with similar results. But he wasn't taking anything larger up there (when I suggested it, he blanched).

The affair proceeded in fits and starts. I had a bit of hero worship and Wes liked sex (having no other outlet). We kept romping in this manner periodically (at least once a week) until I graduated from prep school. And then we had one last fling in New York during winter break, with me traveling down from college and him coming up after a visit to his family in Pennsylvania. I bought tickets to *Mame* and to *Die Meistersinger von Nürnberg* at the Met. He enjoyed the former, suffered through all six hours of the latter, and we destroyed the bed in our hotel room during nights that extended well into late mornings. That February weekend we departed in the midst of a major New York blizzard. We reached LaGuardia, but they had cancelled all flights. We hiked a bit and caught the last bus in sight to the Jackson Heights subway station, the bus driver stopping for us out of sheer compassion (New Yorkers always act tough and gruff, but underneath they have hearts of gold). We took the 7 to Grand Central, and I boarded a train departing for Boston, Wes one to Chicago. We knew this was the last hurrah: "Back to school for you, buddy," his valediction ran.

"See you maybe next summer?"

"If I'm still stationed near you." He hugged me, I imagined in the spirit of comradeship with some shy affection thrown in. I returned the hug out of gratitude for the gift he had given me in becoming a man. After that weekend I never saw him again, and I assumed he would marry and have kids. I had a talent for finding randy, willing, affectionately grateful men, but not for holding on to them, apparently.

That proved equally true when I transferred from my private college to CU, Boulder. I thought I had hit pay dirt the first day with a fellow undergraduate named Carl, whom I met in summer school. He stood a head shorter than I, blond-haired, a wrestler in high school who really knew how to use his compact body in the holds we practiced on overnight campouts. His biceps provided the first attraction, then his legs in hiking shorts. His pecs, lats, and abs all felt as hard as marble, which made me want to inspect his training lower down. His seduction technique (had he read my mind?) lacked subtlety:

"Hey Nick. Do you ever whack off?"

"Well, yes."

"Let's try it together." And then, "Let me try yours and you can try mine." That muscle proved rigidly hard too, jutting out from its triangle of sandy-blond hair, and in this one area I was even more developed than he. Again, no kissing allowed, except on the working parts of the anatomy (with which he exhibited real talent and more than a passing acquaintance). Inserting a finger into his luscious hole also produced spectacular results, but everything else lay out of bounds. He rejected my eager suggestion that he could fit something larger up there: he had met more than his match. Oh well—a quarter of a loaf (or sausage) is better than none.

Carl's father only taught summer school in Boulder, so our romantic interludes were seasonal. I was left to howl at the moon when Carl departed for college in Iowa (where his father held a tenured position in math). Imagining that I was in love, I pined for him in his absence and didn't look for anybody else. We had one more summer's worth of fun before he took his leave, much to my chagrin.

On our last night camping together, holding each other in our sleeping bags, he confessed, "Nick, this has been fun, this summer I mean."

"Sure has!" Did I hope he would transfer from Iowa to Boulder? Make an honest man out of me? I don't know what.

"I'm quitting school and joining the Air Force."

Colorado Springs, I thought, *That'd be great.* But a voice within cautioned against this fantasy.

"I'll be going to basic at Lackland," he prepared me.

"Lackland?"

"Texas, and then to school as a fighter pilot, I hope."

"Great, Carl. Good luck," I replied insincerely. Don't say it: whether they're in uniform or headed for one, I'm a pushover. His bisexuality inclined toward the straight side, but I'm glad he didn't complete the transition before our last summer together. When I saw a picture of him ten years later surrounded by his wife and children, I rejoiced at escaping. Why do straight men become so sloppy when they marry?

After my fantasy of true love departed, given this promising start, you'd think my erotic life would have launched into some deliciously incessant undergraduate promiscuity. No such luck. One night at the end of first semester, junior year, walking down a flight of just four steps to my basement apartment in wet sneakers, I slipped, fell squarely on my back, ruptured a disk, cracked two vertebrae, and landed in an operating room where the doctors relieved the compression of my spinal chord.

Rehabilitation lasted throughout the next year, while I wheeled myself around campus, then swung on crutches, then leaned on a cane, then managed just limping to classes. Throughout my graduate studies every time I slid on an icy path, slept on a soft mattress, or just stepped down the wrong way, I'd wind up in the infirmary of whatever university I was attending. I was not a romantic fellow, given the amount of muscle relaxant and pain killer I was taking. Maybe that's why I did so well at my school work—no side diversions.

When I finally wound up at my last university for a Ph.D., I was too intent on escaping the classroom for any kind of involvement. So I did what any normal red-blooded American boy does in this situation—about five times a day if I could. Good thing I didn't break my right hand in that fall.

A Chosen Landscape

A repressed year abroad followed, which posed the question of whether I really wanted deportation for sex crimes. I did begin, however, to sample a few gay bars in Berlin during my German history fellowship (in allegiance to my mother's Austro-Italian origins, which begot my gray-green irises but curly brown hair). A lot of British, French, and American servicemen percolated though that divided city during those days, and you'd think my proclivities would have led me their way. No such luck. Though I did make a play for a British army lieutenant who, unfortunately, preferred men in uniform as much as I (sporting only the tatty costume of a mere graduate student). By the time I reported to my first teaching post at a major Southern university in the town of Pulpitville, Tennelina, I had locked, loaded, and prepared my musket to shoot at most anything that came into its sights.

Here follows a gay wanderer's song cycle about his earlier years (for you've already seen that lyrics may spill out of my catchall repertory at the drop of a hat). In this genre a young man leaves home for the wider world in search of his fortune and some amorous exploits (perhaps even a mate). If my loosely-knit tale lacks, as these opuses usually do, a central narrative thread (except that provided by the hunt for some roiling carnal delight and a partner), you must piece the "story" together for yourself from a series of episodes glimpsed during the journey. On the way you will view portraits both bizarre and beautiful. Such lyrical fables conclude in one of two ways: with a chanson about arrival in a chosen landscape or about the wayfarer's last end. Enjoy the voyage as far as it goes. I did.

2 IN THE GROVES OF ACADEME

The University of Tennelina in Pulpitville possessed a much-praised and gracious setting in the beautiful layout of its main campus. The planners had wisely preserved the old upper and lower quads, allowing nothing to encroach on their forested expanses. They had consigned the few hideous modernist buildings to the outer fringes of the grounds. And while no other structure had any distinction except for the grotesquely incongruous Pantheon-style central administration building (without any gods in residence, however), the remaining halls of learning fronted on the quads unobtrusively in their red-brick modesty. The only other imposing building, a bell tower in a style borrowed from God knows where, incessantly chimed out Heine's urgent admonition: "We will never meet again so young." It stood as an appropriately phallic portal to a congregation of dormitories where many nubile young men craved release.

The beauty of forested quads, however, offered the sole winning feature of the university, the surrounding town, and its 45,000-odd permanent residents (emphasis on "odd"), consisting mostly of faculty members or the families of faculty members. Pulpitville, its university, and its denizens (students and townspeople alike) specialized in an empty pretension to an "old Southern" legacy they didn't possess. A friend of mine from a state in the deep South liked to call this "Tennelina twee," which hit the mark squarely. True, the town had incorporated during the Federalist era. But it featured a seedy main street, "historic" 1930s houses decaying into not-so-genteel shabbiness, and inhabitants who matched their dwellings. Tennelina never boasted a planter aristocracy like that in some Southern states. The people who claimed descent from "old Southern families" had forbears who generally arrived on American shores "transported" from England to avoid hanging and to decrease the surplus population of pickpockets, thieves, fences, prostitutes, and highwaymen (had nobody in Pulpitville ever read *Moll Flanders*?).

To give just a few examples of the prevailing Southern charade, the university president's "mansion," with its pillared plantation veranda, had originated in a mail-order catalog from the old Southern town of Cleveland, Ohio, the pre-manufactured components shipped by rail and assembled on site. The faculty likewise migrated from northern universities such as Harvard, Yale, or Chicago and most of the graduate students came from New England or the Midwest. Tennelina natives regarded all northerners indiscriminately as "Yankees." I disabused one of the more vocal natives firmly on this point by observing that I was a Midwesterner, and one from the Land of Lincoln at that. "Not to worry," I added, "We don't plan to burn down any more houses in town, at least, not this week"—a reference to the occupation of Pulpitville during the "War (diphthong: Woe-ah) of Northern Aggression."

You can see by now that the Southern Mystique exerted no hold on me. The Civil War had ended more than a century before, though you couldn't tell from some of my Southern colleagues and a few of the fleeting boyfriends, whose failure to acknowledge this simple fact brought those relationships to a speedy conclusion. Nostalgia for some vision of an old South that none of their families had experienced (unless dirt farming constituted plantation life) bordered on the macabre. I once infuriated an older gay friend by suggesting, after being lectured about Southern etiquette, that he cast the members of his circle in a transvested version of *Gone with the Wind*. The question remained, as in 1939, who would play Scarlett? My friend knew plenty of "actresses," but no British ones. Fiddledeedee! "There're only Yankees and damn Yankees," another of my Pulpitville acquaintances declared vehemently. Knowing that he meant northerners in general, I inquired delicately about the difference. The bitter rejoinder came back, "The damn Yankees *stay!* If it weren't for air conditionin', y'all wouldn't be here." And you could see he believed it, because he refused to modernize his extravagantly dilapidated "historic-district" house, which consequently nurtured a rich black mold throughout its walls.

Pulpitville cultivated a backward-looking perspective nourished by the myth of Tennelina exceptionalism, which amounted to nothing more than Southern nativism in the last analysis. I encountered this xenophobia immediately, when two of my Tennelina-born colleagues walked up to me on my first day and announced that they hadn't wanted to hire another "foreigner" to teach nineteenth-century German history. I could save myself a lot of anguish, they gave it expressly to be known, by leaving sooner rather than later, preferably on the next bus out of town. Not a semester passed when this advice didn't resurface in one way or another. And I, for my part, answered by incessantly popping the bubbles blown by my more hidebound fellow professors, most of whom were "extinct volcanoes"—faculty who had published once and then never again after receiving tenure.

The University's exclusive honorary societies existed specifically to reinforce the general xenophobia—societies such as the Knights of the Silver Mohair and the Order of the Honorable Possum (induction awarded to Southern professors who could play dead convincingly throughout faculty meetings). Since these organizations only included good ol' boys, most faculty never beheld their mumbo jumbo. But rumor had it that meetings featured self-congratulatory toasts and traditional minstrel numbers such as:

> O! we used to have fun on the ol' plantation,
> We used to have fun on the ol' plantation,
> We used to have fun on the ol' plantation,
>   Way down in the Tenn'line State.
> O! we danced an' sang when the day's work's over
> Lived like kings in the fields of clover,
> Sang to the Dean when he was sober,
>   An' it's he's very rich an' great.
>   [Chorus]
> An' it's by an' by we do hope to meet him,
> An' it's by an' by we do hope to meet him,
> An' it's by an' by we do hope to meet him,
>   Down in the Tenn'line State.

The drink of choice was bourbon and branch water (society bylaws banned Manhattans). Whether they danced the Tennelina Reel on these occasions lay open to debate, since a large number of the brethren stood a little heavy on their trotters.

The Southern-born president of the University began his introduction to new faculty, "Look to the right of you and to the left. None of you will be here in seven years." He should just have mounted a framed "Yankees Go Home" sampler in his office. Our inevitable departure was *his* fantasy. When he resigned in disgrace as a result of a cheating scandal a few years later, I wanted to send him a note consisting of one word, *Vaffanculo!* But I thought better of it: his command of foreign languages was as limited as his megalomania was extensive.

That peculiarly descriptive Italian profanity could also have referred to another feature of Pulpitville University accompanying its involuted xenophobia: a pervasive homophobia lurking beneath a tissue-thin veneer of liberalism. I lived openly gay, my WASP name, Nicholas Walker, contravened by my Italianate features. I therefore stood guilty on three counts: "abnormal" sexuality, "suspect" ethnicity, and (worst of all) northern patrimony. Though I performed my duties too well to brook direct challenge, certain barriers to "my kind" would always exist. Unless they were superb scholars and excellent teachers, openly gay men had difficulty gaining tenure or promotion to full professor, let alone becoming "named professors" (usually reserved for those servile enough to have their academic vacuity overlooked in trade for an extra stipend). And though administrative positions generally provided refuge to failed researchers (the level of appointment directly proportional to the degree of fatuity), those gay men who craved executive power could never become dean, provost, or president of the University. In fact, openly gay men rarely served as departmental chairs—only two that I can recall during my years of service. This pervasive homophobia produced bizarre marriages of convenience, which a few salient examples will suffice to illustrate.

In my own department resided one of the most subtle and pernicious members of the down-low fraternity, a professor named Robert Hastings, whom I shall call Little Boy Blue (because he always dressed in jeans and a blue denim shirt and jacket). His garb, together with his long gray ponytail, survived as a relic of the proclivity among many faculty active during the early 70s to affect student costume. In Little Boy's case this meant junior-high garb, for he stood no more than 4'10, about the level of my chest. He was one of the charmers who suggested on my first day that I depart immediately, and he reinforced this periodically by placing notes in my faculty mailbox about other positions: "Nick, you should apply," they usually read.

His hostility derived in part from his lack of success. Both students and colleagues disliked him, and he hadn't published anything noteworthy during his entire academic career. But his nastiness toward me also had its roots in envy of an openly gay man (I initially brought boyfriends to faculty parties) and fear of anybody who might be acquainted with his extracurricular activities. For Little Boy liked to exercise his sexual proclivities discretely, which is to say, in New York, where he would persuade former graduate students to serve as pimps. Not surprisingly, he possessed a strong vein of sadism, and what sort of trade his former students procured for him I cannot begin to imagine. He also spent a good deal of his New York sojourns in the baths and grungier sex clubs, where he presented himself as much younger in the gloom ("He could very well pass for forty-two, in the dusk with the light behind him"—refrain repeated by chorus of naked lads). He later shuffled off this mortal coil at the Eastside Baths from a surfeit of poppers. His wife knew nothing of his side activities, and he made sure that she didn't attend the quaint faculty "sherries" to socialize with colleagues who might drop indiscrete hints.

This same obliviousness blessed the wife of an older and somewhat musty professor in the philosophy department named Giles Barnard, who had a nickname among the students: The Stripper. He basked in the prestige of his wife's "old Tennelina family," and he liked to do that basking in the buff among various locales on campus. Rumor, mostly untrue, had it that he exposed himself on the quads at night. But I encountered him prowling the locker rooms shared by students and faculty in the gym. If he spied something he liked, he would immediately strip down to take a shower (he never actually participated in athletic activities). If I intended to work out and he appeared in the locker room, I'd cancel my session for the day to avoid his intrusive gaze and the sight of his sagging skin the color and texture of cracked, brown shoe leather.

For sheer ugliness, though, a gay-but-married faculty member from the English Department beat The Stripper cold. Aloysius Throckmorton bore a stunning resemblance to the frog footman in *Alice in Wonderland* (more amazingly, his wife was a dead ringer for the Duchess). How Frogman, his notorious sobriquet, seduced his students I never fathomed. Perhaps he put a bag over his head for his down-low rutting. It became a standing joke among the graduates and undergraduates in English that a "conference" in his office entailed a plunge beneath his desk. Did he exchange grades for their acquiescence? I couldn't imagine any other arrangement that would have procured him sex, but I would discover further details later in my career.

Chief psychiatric honors among the gay Pulpitville demimonde went unquestionably to campus chaplain Grant Downing, a.k.a Leather Minister, whose fulltime job involved presiding over one of the local congregations. A tall, slim, handsome young man in his mid 30s, he resembled a wholesome 1950s matinee idol in a clerical collar, with a shock of dark brown hair, a doting group of female admirers in his flock, and a mousy wife. On Sundays he preached to his congregation, and during the week he tended the spiritual needs of students. But on Friday evenings he attended gay parties in a neighboring town, clad in leather harness boots, leather chaps that revealed his substantial endowments front and back, a leather buckle harness that crossed his bare chest, a leather biker's cap, and matching bondage wrist bands. He reputedly carried a leather flail with him to these events (I never actually attended one). At some point in the evening he would retire to a bedroom set up for the purpose, throw his legs up in a leather sling, and offer the whole company the opportunity to watch and participate as various partygoers whipped him, had him in any way they wished (so long as it involved rough group configurations), and otherwise abused him.

How Leather Minister hid his stripes from his wife I'll never understand. But in the end he had to relinquish the charade of his marriage and also his position. For just as he liked to be abused, so he enjoyed beating his spouse when he drank at home. Finally one night she fielded a pistol from his desk drawer and offered to alter his genitals permanently if he raised his hand to her again. In consequence of this rebellion he filed a complaint, divorced her, and found a new congregation far, far away. Some flock must have fit his talents, but I never heard where.

Only Quentin Warner exceeded Leather Minister as a grotesque in the menagerie of fraud. He was also known in certain circles as Blimpy, the University organist (in several senses of the word). He gave morbid obesity a bad name: fat tumbled down his rotundity, gathering in pouches that fell into his pants. He didn't so much walk as waddle from side to side, tilting his immense weight first to one side and then to the other for perambulation. Lard pervaded his whole being, encasing his tiny eyes in oily pastries, bloating his cheeks and his lips (which almost hid his rodent-like central incisors), then cascading down his neck in multitudinous chins that resembled massive goiters. His wife, unfortunately, became aware of his activities with men, because she couldn't fail to notice how much time he spent with the lads who turned pages for him at recitals (one could only practice so much—at least music). As an organist he possessed vast knowledge of pipes, wind chests, and blowers, or so the story ran.

Blimpy's last appearance on the concert stage offered a memorable finale to his career, with its own chapter in University lore. He lumbered slowly out to the organ, sat himself on the groaning bench, and delivered a program consisting entirely of Bach (fittingly

Baroque). While he sweated like a whole hog at a barbecue, his bloated arms loomed ominously over the keyboard and his disproportionately dainty feet tapped out a dance on the pedals. He ended with the monumental fugue sometimes called "St. Anne," because its initial subject coincidentally resembles that of the tune to "O God, Our Help in Ages Past," often sung at funerals. Certainly at Blimpy's, for about halfway through a very loud passage he suffered a fatal coronary and collapsed on the live keyboard, bringing all the pipes into play. Bach's music suddenly transformed itself into modernist experimentalism. Some thought divine justice had been served, especially his wife, who for the first time in memory (and perhaps her whole marriage) cracked a covert, quickly suppressed smile.

A few courageous souls decided their marriages of convenience perpetrated a sham, choosing divorce and life with a gay partner instead. They paid a price for their honesty in Pulpitville, but they formed the exception that proved the rule.

My point in sketching just a few of the more colorful denizens of this chamber of horrors (call it Walker's Waxworks, if you will) lies simply in displaying what I profoundly didn't wish to become: a prisoner in Pulpitville's twilit world. Better to live in the full light of day, whatever the consequences (which I would only realize later). Finding companionship, though, presented the problem at hand. And the answers seemed to come from searching the few gay bars and discos in the area. This initially meant negotiating the transient world of students, undergraduate and graduate.

At the time I began university teaching I was in my twenties, only a couple of years older than the undergraduates and younger than many of my graduate students. That made me fair game for student attention, I discovered. A basic rule applied, however: "Thou shalt keep thy privates out of the cash register" (let's just call this the First Great Commandment of university life). In other words, no playing with undergraduates in one's classes, even when they made passes, which in my first years they often did. It occasionally happened that I dallied with a former student no longer in my academic charge. But if I encountered an erstwhile paramour in class, I pretended awkwardly not to recognize him. "And the Second Commandment is like unto it: Thou shalt not fraternize with undergraduates of any persuasion in thy department." (Purely social association with departmental graduate students proved a different matter.) Not all faculty, gay or straight, followed this second directive, but prudence recommended it for reasons both practical and emotional.

Other habitués of gay locales sometimes came from the towns surrounding Pulpitville, but there weren't many of that odd sort. Most gay men who chose to live long-term in the Bible Belt had partners, and affairs with them entailed the same problem as with married men. Somebody in the threesome was liable to be shafted, figuratively more than literally. Such a ménage never resulted in a good outcome, not that I didn't make my share of mistakes. But let's take the cases as they come, beginning with graduate students.

3 A SEPARATE TRUCE

In the gay haunts around Pulpitville, in the bars, discos, and clubs beyond the town limits and in nearby cities, I could not avoid my own graduate students. More than that, Barker Commons, the apartment development where I initially rented, had a large collection of gay graduate students (birds of a feather?), a number from my department but others from outside it. When I first entered the modest gay disco on the edge of town, I caused a small exodus, several of my students slinking away. It soon became apparent that we needed to find a way to coexist where we resided and partied. We couldn't just pretend that we didn't all occupy the same spaces, whether it be the laundry room or the dance floor.

After the initial embarrassment passed, we hit on an unspoken treaty that all of us honored scrupulously: in the confines of the History Department we pretended we didn't know each other outside of work. Neither did we ever engage in what the University lexicon politely labeled "intradepartmental amorous encounters." But in the apartment complex we intermingled as a group of about nine, including roommates (I lived alone initially). And if I engaged with one of the latter (all of whom came from outside the History Department), he came over to my place for extracurricular activities. Of course, any graduate students outside of the Department were fair game, and that provided my first bit of fun after years of unhappy celibacy.

Parry, a delectable biology grad student, shared a place in the Commons with Duncan, a Southerner and one of my more louche master's degree candidates. Parry and Duncan slip-streamed off one another. If one of them brought home some luscious bit of male pulchritude from a club or cruising spot, the victorious hunter (after the desired utilization) would donate to the other, but never in three-ways—their particular roommate treaty.

Parry found himself unaccompanied by his roommate one Sunday night at the club when I wandered in. Apparently he had me in his sights, and he used the oldest and easiest pickup technique in the book: he bought me one drink, then another. I didn't need much persuading to invite him back to my place (he *was* cute), and he began my education.

To my delight, and unlike any previous man I had encountered, Parry liked foreplay, especially kissing with a lot of heavy tongue. He did this so well that if we had gone on any longer, I think I would have let loose before I took my clothes off. In the nick of time, though, he escorted me to the bathroom, stripped me, and we both stepped into the shower. Soaping each other down aroused me again. He knew well what he wanted to do after that, and he retained a categorical knowledge of all the techniques at his command. Having wrapped a towel around my waist, he guided me into the bedroom, pulled back the spread and commanded me to lie down. He pulled my towel off, looked over the equipment, and quipped succinctly, "Excellent!" Parry had what I can only describe as an ultra-deep throat, and I thought to myself, *You're superb, but is there more?* It turns out he was just fluffing.

A Chosen Landscape

Parry's ultimate goal lay in getting truly and thoroughly stuffed; I stood (so to speak) at the portals of the promised land. From his pants on the floor he fetched a bottle of poppers (another first for me), took a snort, asked me to try some, and then reached for the lube. With us both greased, he lowered himself gingerly onto me, "Need to take it easy at first—a lot to handle." It's difficult to describe adequately the feeling of that gloriously tight fit the first time you find it, and Parry sat terrifically in the saddle. He became so magnificently stiff, with his balls repeatedly brushing the lower outcropping of my tight brown curls, that I could have hung my laundry from him. Inspired, I couldn't wait to touch, not look, but when I reached out to stroke him, he cautioned, "Careful, man—I'm really close." We almost climaxed together: I flooded him and he launched with such force, that his cream splattered the wall behind the headboard. We both watched in amazement as his copious sap dripped slowly down the off-white paint. He leaned over for a kiss, panting from the exertion, but he didn't dismount, just smiled at me, "How many more times can you do this tonight?"

"I don't know," I replied. "Let's find out."

> Come again! Sweet love doth now invite
> Thy graces that refrain
> To do me due delight.
> To see, to hear, to touch, to kiss, to die
> With thee again in sweetest sympathy.

As Parry slunk away at 4 AM, I recalled the last stanza:

> Gentle love, draw forth thy wounding dart,
> Thou canst not touch his heart;
> For I that do approve
> By sighs and tears more hot than are thy shafts
> Did tempt while he for triumph laughs.

Draw forth thy wounding dart, indeed. We weren't in love, just in lust. We both knew that he would move on in a couple of years, and we hadn't the remotest intention of any close relationship. But he became a sporadic buddy who called occasionally for a little mutual fulfillment. He enjoyed the role of a dedicated bottom boy (catcher, if you will), and it turned out that, with a couple of significant exceptions, I liked playing the position of dedicated pitcher. Occasionally Parry let me taste the ample results of his arousal (prefaced by the plea, "Don't stop!"). He eventually went off to a job in San Francisco, where I suppose the natives found him as talented as I did.

Other interesting catchers from that period included the mercurial Daren (taking a masters in botany). I met him in a neighboring town at some mutual acquaintances' large gay party to which Daren had come as one of the hosts' date for the evening. He chatted with me for a little while, and then asked disingenuously, "Would you like to see my apartment—it's nearby." We left the party for about an hour, only to slink back unobserved, or so we imagined. Not so: the whole throng, or at least those who had not locked themselves in one of the bathrooms or bedrooms for some recreation, had assembled to receive us. The fellow who invited Daren exclaimed to the multitude, "Well, you two, where have you been?" And then to Daren,

"You were supposed to be my date," which elicited a rejoinder from somebody at the back of the room, "But he came as my date!" Nobody held this against us, apparently, for I became part of the honorary family, invited to the "After Brunch," where we continued with Bloody Marys, Belgian waffles, and a full review of the evening's proceedings, trick by trick. The group recounted the details of my and Daren's sudden absence and reappearance in vivid detail, and this actually raised my standing considerably within the cohort.

During our weirdly sporadic encounters, which persisted for about a year, Daren could never quite decide whether he wanted to visit on a given night or not. He would ask for a date, and then at the last minute decide he'd rather cruise the bars than come to my place. When he did commit to a night of play, however, he kept urging, "Harder, harder," coining a sobriquet for me that stuck among my fellows: Thumper.

In a somewhat more casual vein lay Robert, living in the next building over, a scrumptious little tart who had abandoned his quest for a Ph.D. in favor of an M.B.A. Robert believed neither in dates nor in foreplay: he'd simply ring the bell, walk in, close the door, pull down his pants, bend over, and say, "I'm ready." I generally was too. Several other catchers tracked through our community, some part of our immediate social circle, others itinerant but willing fellow travelers who visited from time to time.

The gentlemen's agreement between the graduate-student residents of Barker Commons persisted for the two or three years we all lived there. I remember particularly, for example, a shared road trip we took to tea dance about 30 miles away in a neighboring city on a late Sunday afternoon. At the dance an older man with a young friend in tow picked me up, and when I disappeared, my companions drove home without me (knowing that I was otherwise engaged). I seduced the young friend easily, and after spending a sleepless night with him, begged a ride back to Pulpitville at 6 AM. I showered, donned tie and coat, and somehow made it through the day's teaching. My graduate students politely ignored my nodding head in class, and our separate truce continued. In truth, they were a decent lot and very kind to me. I had just arrived in the program and in town; they had all been there several years. None of them ever sought gain from our acquaintance, though they could have spread nasty and all-too-true rumors about me around the Department. But they observed our unwritten treaty, perhaps with the thought that I could drop a couple of dimes on them too. We gossiped richly, commenting on each other's affairs and tricks, but only among ourselves.

From among the group of graduate students in Barker Common came one of the most precious relationships among homosexual men: a gay best friend. Andrew (an Anglicization of Andrei) Ivanov descended from Russian nobility who had fled the October Revolution and who retained long memory of their aristocratic heritage. Andrew had strikingly blond Slavic good looks, with deep-set blue eyes, and he matched my height almost exactly (6'1) and age (27 when we first met). We coincidentally attended the same church, he out of loyalty to his upbringing as an Episcopalian (there being no Russian Orthodox Church where he grew up), I fleeing censorious Roman Catholicism and its musical dreariness (for I sang occasionally with the town's glorious Episcopal choir). Noticing this and the fact that we were neighbors, Andrew invited me to a party of all his gay friends, after which he suggested we take a romp. I can truthfully say we had the worst sex of my life, which mercifully lasted only a half an hour before both of us gave up. He had a decent body but no discernable talent. As these things go, discarded tricks often become friends, and given our common interests—cooking, clubbing, entertaining, the arts, literature, religion—we soon became close confidants.

Andrew had many idiosyncratic traits, one of which lay in his undying fealty to the remnants of the Romanov dynasty (one of his great grandfathers or other had served as a government minister during the waning days of the Empire). His family stayed in touch with some members of the Imperial House, and Andrew awaited like the Second Coming the return to the throne of the Grand Duke Vladimir Kirillovich, then claimant to the title of Tsar and Autocrat of all the Russias. This expectation exuded a pronounced air of fantasy, but Andrew took it seriously. And he carried himself somewhat ceremoniously, as if he might someday inherit his father's traditional titles. This earned him the sobriquet "Grand Duchess Anastasia" among the more cynical in our crowd. But I regarded this delusion as intriguing, because Andrew was in fact both harmless and very well educated (he had taken his undergraduate degree at Harvard, and his father was a professor of French at a small Midwestern college).

Andrew's eccentricity entailed another peculiarity: a constant and pervasive hypochondria. He claimed to have been diagnosed at one time with some terrible lower intestinal syndrome. Suspiciously, though, it disappeared when he came out, leading me to believe that he was simply nervous in the service about being gay. He called not infrequently to have me retrieve from the pharmacy this or that prescription, none of which I examined to see whether they treated a real physical malaise or just neurosis. Along with his other idiosyncrasies, Andrew's real or imagined maladies could have irritated, but they struck me then (and still do) as part of gay life's fascination. Andrew's company entertained in curious and unexpected ways.

Not to mention the fact that Andrew cooked virtuosically. For his circle of friends he would begin with amazing French soups or *blinis Demidov* (in memory of the Russian prince), followed by *tournedos à la Rossini* with *sauce Béarnaise* (Lord knows where he found the *foie gras* and truffles for this), or *poulet rôti à la Normande*, *coq au vin*, *caneton à l'orange*, or *homard thermidor*, with *gratin Dauphinois* or *pommes Anna* and succulent vegetables. He followed these with a green salad, then port and Stilton, finishing with a slice of (what else?) *charlotte Malakoff*. For one first course he triumphed with a whole poached salmon served cold and glazed in a shining aspic: genius and artistry conjoined to produce legend! Occasionally we would collaborate on cheese and grape receptions with assorted wines and champagne. I suspect all this rich food contributed to Andrew's digestive woes, but I had no quarrel with an exquisite meal.

Andrew enrolled as a doctoral candidate in Italian, which language and literature he adored, and we naturally formed the kind of bond that exists between students of German and Italian (just read Mann's *Tonio Kröger* or *Death in Venice*). My heritage combined both northern and southern strains, which fashioned a sturdy foundation for our friendship. Andrew's study of Italian followed certain proclivities, and he liked to move around his apartment singing to himself and smiling lubriciously as he went (I translate):

> The white and sweet swan
> Dies singing,
> As I do, weeping,
> Toward the end of my life.
> Strange and diverse fate:
> That he dies disconsolate,
> And I die blessed.
> Death that in dying
> Fills me completely with joy and desire;
> Because in dying I feel no further sadness,
> I would gladly die a thousand times a day.

Andrew dedicated himself to the role of bottom, longing always for a "complete filling."

Since I knew the members of his department but distantly, I served as sounding board for his complaints about the politics of his faculty, which he viewed with a Slavic eye for conspiracy. He imagined a plot against his progress at every turn in his relationship to his advisor and to other faculty members.

"Farinelli has it in for me," he would voice his paranoia.

"First, Farinelli isn't on your doctoral committee. Second, I'll bet that his colleagues don't think all that highly of him, though I don't know for sure. Third, he only notices that you're blond, blue-eyed, and handsome. That might do you some good, because he's just slightly more queer than a three dollar bill, if that's possible. And finally, I can tell you from experience that no professor cares as much about you as you do about yourself" (which in my experience was generally true in all departments). But no graduate student ever believes that he doesn't lie at the center of his academic universe, an axiom that extends to most of us.

During nights out on the town Andrew made for a charming, comely, and lively compatriot, replete with a full store of gossip about our acquaintances inside and outside the gay community. Over dinner prepared by one or the other of us, we traded tales, wide-eyed, for at least a thousand and one nights, of our amorous adventures and intrigue, of the boys we had just bedded or wanted to, of the parties we would attend in the weeks to come.

"Saw you leave with that accountant last night," Andrew would offer by way of pumping me for information in a typical conversation. "Did you go home with him?"

"How would you know he's an accountant?"

"Everybody knows he's an accountant. He's tallied up a lot of numbers, I hear."

"We're being vicious today, my friend? We spent the night together. Objections?"

"Please. It's also a matter of common knowledge that he's a china queen who has a larger collection of Imari than Duke Alexandre of Lorraine once assembled."

"We're not on the Russian imperial family again?"

"No. More distant relatives—the Hapsburgs."

"Of course," I paused skeptically, continuing realistically, "You're just fishing for details from last night."

"I certainly am. What else?"

"Then you'll need to see for yourself. But basically he's collected nothing more exotic than Wedgwood and Waterford, and that characterization extends to the owner, who has about as much personality as his crockery. I don't think he's your type, anyhow."

"Really? Tell me in excruciating detail."

"Well, he likes pretty much what you like, so you'd need to become a switch hitter. And he's extremely passive . . . I wanted to check for a pulse. Still, if you're tending toward necrophilia, he may amuse you."

"Got up on the wrong side of the bed? Snarky mood?"

"Serves you right for prying. Now, about that party next Saturday you've been invited to. May I tag along?"

"But of course."

Andrew was a good sounding board, and when one or the other of us wasn't dating somebody, we went out together on Wednesday, Friday, and Saturday nights. Following our weekend pub crawl, we sometimes accompanied each other to the 5:30 "whore's mass" (for those undergraduate and graduate students who partied into the wee hours of the Sunday morning and didn't arise until early afternoon).

Andrew and I appeared so often at the bars and discos together (though usually driving separate cars, should opportunity knock), that many considered us lovers. In a sense, he was more important than a lover. The latter came and went at more or less frequent intervals in those first years. Gay best friends last forever, or at least until they go off to Rome for study abroad and never return, as in Andrew's case. After his research grant expired, he managed to stay on for decade after decade, living God knows how. I visited him in his digs there during a couple of European jaunts, and he seemed to do just fine on no visible means of support. I didn't ask any questions. We've lost touch now; I wonder what became of him?

Through Andrew and my immediate group of graduate-student friends I met others, and amid affairs that lasted months, I embarked on the much more serious first adventure of living with somebody. I began with Calder (Cal) Blount, who moved into my apartment at Barker Commons during my second full year of residence. He offered my first experience of anything resembling gay domesticity.

4 HOUSEMATES WITH BENEFITS

It's safe to say that Calder Blount, despite his imposingly traditional Anglo-Saxon name—or perhaps because if it—was the most exotic creature I had encountered to that point in my limited gay experience. He had grown up in northern Virginia, the adopted only child of very unassuming parents, who, however, had made a small fortune when a developer purchased their farmland to feed the suburban appetite for housing around Washington D.C. They once came to visit, speaking in the accents of the rural South, a patois that Cal didn't remotely share. Is there a word for gay inflection in speech, the one that allows us to identify a fellow church member upon first hearing, that summons instinctual recognition? Can we call the dialect "gayese"? I doubt it—perhaps we should designate it "the lilt" (no lisp involved, by the way—that's a myth generated by forward "s"). Whatever its label, "upspeak" discovered a past master in Cal.

His parents doted on their son, giving him anything and everything he wanted and indulging his every peculiar whim. But they always appeared somewhat bewildered, like farmyard chickens who sat on an egg that hatched a falcon. How did these good, homely country folk produce so fey a creature, which, moreover, confronted them with its outré style of life and adventures as inevitabilities that they accepted without apparent demur? In some sense, though for different reasons, I was as entranced and astonished as they. I too came from Cal's suburban background, but he had absorbed gay culture with a ferocious precocity that continually astounded.

He stood about 5'11 when I first met him on the dance floor, which turned out to be his natural habitat. He wore a pair of great round tortoiseshell spectacles that clearly disclosed brown eyes underneath wavy brown hair cut to a moderate length, and he possessed a boyish figure clad in alabaster skin. He continually bore an expression of amazement and complicity, as if he always had some secret to impart or receive in the service of a mischievous plot. His constant patter of gossip and rumor entertained, as silly at it could sometimes be.

Beneath Cal's supercilious exterior, however, lay the admirable traits of great intelligence, keen perception, and serious diligence. As a graduate student in French, he often used a pickup line from a song just then au courant, "Voulez-vous coucher avec moi ce soir?" When he first directed the invitation to me in complete sincerity, he had researched my proclivities, talents, and endowments thoroughly. For although Cal possessed the equipment (and, God knows, overabundant energy) befitting a highly successful pitcher, he was as dedicated and enthusiastic a catcher as ever I've encountered (and that's saying a lot). He also danced with a devotion and talent that stood in direct contrast to my self-conscious clumsiness. When Cal whisked me off the disco floor that first night and into my bedroom, he said quite plainly after we had romped, "Well, the grapevine got that one right, Thumper." I tried insincerely to muster a look of incomprehension at this comment, but he could immediately uncover any imposture on my part. He lived by the wisdom he embodied:

The World is a Bubble and full of Decoys,
Her glittering Pleasures are flattering Boys;
The which in themselves no true Happiness brings,
Rich Rubies, nay Diamonds, Chains, Jewels and Rings:
They are but as Dross, and in Time will decay,
So will Virgin Beauty, tho' ever so gay.

Cal was completely and utterly wanton, and he served as an excellent, worldly-wise pilot through the shoals of urban gay life. That is to say, he knew D.C.—the nearest real city to Pulpitville—like the back of his hand, and he began our friendship by inviting me to tour all the gay watering holes with him. In those days these mostly centered on P Street just off Dupont Circle, and included Mr. P's (bar with tenebrous backroom), The Frat House (bar with video-screened semi-backroom where one could grope very intimately and surreptitiously indulge in oral sports on occasion), Friends (piano bar with an older crowd), Rascals (on Connecticut Avenue just above the Circle—multi-tiered, with the upper floors given over to young male strippers) and the holy of holies, Badlands (new, with many dance floors). D.C. also offered P-Street Beach, a set of trails into the woods above Rockland Park where men had sex in the open, and then a strip club next to a bathhouse in the seamier precincts of Southwest. Nothing like this existed around Pulpitville, but with Cal as my companion and guide, I discovered a whole new kind of gay existence.

I learned quickly, and I practiced as much as I could to make perfect: "fabu" (as Cal was wont to exclaim)!

Cal unhappily shared a small dorm room when we met, he had a bit of thing for me (but only a bit), and thus he suggested he move into my second bedroom, "So, Nick, what would you think of splitting your place?"

"What's in it for me? Don't get me wrong, I like you well enough, Cal. But I haven't had a roommate since I was an undergraduate."

"Not 'roommate'; housemate. I'd shoulder half the rent, utilities, and phone bill—don't pretend that you're all that well paid as an assistant professor."

He had a point about the financial side of this: my department chair was a skinflint who regarded his ability to hire faculty members on the cheap as one of his virtues. He didn't understand that he engendered disloyalty in this way, but that wouldn't become apparent for quite some time in my case. So I replied to Cal, "All right, let's try it out. We'll either get along or not, though I do have some reservations."

Now, Cal trolled around Pulpitville for multiple liaisons (I was just one, though a favorite). We maintained no illusions that we would develop some sort of "relationship," neither did we "sleep" together in the conventional sense of the word. But when it suited him, if we went out dancing, he might wind up in my bed for the night We weren't merely housemates, but housemates with benefits.

And the benefits (aside from easily available sexual gratification)? At first considerable. I liked to cook menus he liked to eat. He liked to wash dishes, clean, and iron, all of which he did obsessively. I tended toward neatness. But Cal possessed more detergent solutions and housekeeping equipment than a professional maid service for sweeping, scrubbing, dusting, shampooing the carpets, washing the bathroom, laundering the bed linens (he'd bring mine back with a knowing wink, "we've been a very active boy, haven't we?"), and disinfecting the kitchen. Ironing was his true passion, including our underwear, polo shirts, and even the permanent-press sheets—he would not bear anything unpressed against his delicate skin. He used my cologne, I used his. We entertained together, both the grad students in Barker Commons, friends of mine, friends of his, and the various other strays who wandered through the apartment. He invited me to student parties; I invited him to the few gay faculty dinner parties that cropped up from time to time. In some sense, then, we were occasional bedmates keeping house together in a fluid pattern that involved friendship, not love. That worked well for about a semester.

First there came the problem of our not-so-mutual acquaintances. I discovered the ne plus ultra among Cal's circle in Morton, his D.C. boyfriend. I had not known about this arrangement until Cal moved in, and jealousy never occurred to me. But it did to Morton. I had to endure aggravating phone conversations with him, which typically ran (when I unfortunately intercepted a call meant for Cal):

"Hello, this is Morton," fully confirmed by his obnoxious nasal whine. "Where's Cal?"

"Out," came my deliberately unsatisfactory reply.

"Out where?"

"How should I know?"

"Oh, you *know*," he insinuated, followed by "Have you been fucking my boyfriend?"

The truthful response to this would have run, "A little less than you, since he visits you every other weekend—certainly not as much as the rest of the gay students on campus, whom he entertains on a seminightly basis, sometimes two in an evening." Morton worked as an accountant and probably didn't own a pistol, I imagined. He lived, moreover, a good three hours' drive from us. Still, it seemed prudent to lie, "No, I haven't been 'fucking your boyfriend'—that's your job." Not the most diplomatic reply. If Morton had desired exclusive possession, he should have quit his D.C. job and moved to Pulpitville. But this would have deprived Cal of a D.C. base that didn't involve his parents (who had no inkling of his extraordinary promiscuity, even though they knew, as did *tout le monde*, about his sexual orientation). Cal surely didn't wish to surrender his urban prowling (and that, I believe, provided the motivation behind his continuing liaison with whiney Morton). Morton would inevitably hang up after my rude quip. This usually led to a somewhat testy exchange between Cal and me, in which he deplored my dealings with Morton and I maintained a profound willingness to give up any and all encounters with the fellow for the rest of recorded time.

Only slightly less irritating was Cal's fellow graduate student in French and best gay friend, Barton, whom we more or (in my case) less affectionately knew as Barry. Barry's attraction to Cal puzzled me a bit at first: Barry came from trailer trash just as surely as Cal came from money. But Barry's motives weren't mercenary.

Instead, he recognized something "country" in Cal's roots, however little they showed. Barry represented Cal's Southern alter ego, which made him anathema to me.

Barry's other failings were vividly apparent. Most young men have a certain physical attractiveness that comes from gilded youth, and gay men usually pay some attention to their appearance. Not Barry. The fairy presiding over his birth thrashed him soundly with the ugly stick, endowing him with a flattened face, a weak chin, and skin that looked like he had contracted a disfiguring case of smallpox—recently. He had a disposition that fit his looks: dyspeptic, envious, and perfidious.

When I asked Cal what he found at all entertaining about Barry, the answer came back simply, "He can dance." And truly the boy performed like a ballet star at the disco, though the choreography didn't remotely resemble anything classical. Cal was a dance maven and Barry his partner: Ginger and Fred reincarnated without taffeta and tails.

Barry wanted Cal to himself (he had a crush), and he went out of his way to encourage our every disagreement. He never realized that my "relationship" with Cal extended merely to housemates with benefits and a certain amount of fun we had together (we both loved antiquing, and Cal knew every gay dealer in a seventy mile radius). The "benefits" made Barry jealous, for he never had sex with Cal. And I was by far the more comely and prestigious armpiece: "Look at the gorgeous young professor I snagged," I could imagine my housemate telling his gay friends, most of whom I started avoiding.

Housemates with Benefits

It came to the point that when Barry paid Cal a visit, I would find some excuse to leave. Cal finally caught on to this: if he wanted the place to himself, he had only to announce the impending arrival of the little troll. As he'd walk in the door, I'd exit, "So very nice to see you, Barry. Sorry I can't stay." Neither of us felt the slightest regret.

Cal later commented, "Why are you always the most polite to people you can't stand?"

"It saves me telling them what I really think. Isn't there some way you can get Barry, say, three years of complimentary plastic surgery? It might help, though it's a long shot."

"That's very unkind. He didn't bargain for the face he inherited anymore than you did."

"True, but he could help his venomous personality."

"You don't like my friends."

"No, and I'm not required to. Remember: just 'housemates.'"

Neither did Cal, to be fair, much fancy my friends. He found Andrew's hypochondria tiresome and his Russian fantasies ridiculous, "He's living in Never-Neverland if he thinks the Russians are going to reinstate some sort of aristocracy or monarchy."

"Well, it's a monarchy in exile."

"They're the descendents of deposed princelings ready for nothing more than a good long stay in a psych ward. Do they still drive cabs?" Cal had me there: Andrew was just this side of certifiable, or perhaps he had crossed that line.

"It's amusing and harmless. Anyhow, who among us fancies himself queen of the disco?"

"At least I'm a living monarch. The 'Grand Duchess' is boring, and by the way, thoroughly dead, I hear, from the waist down. That includes his dancing. I've seen more animated Russian nesting dolls."

Cal also disliked the few gay Pulpitville couples of my acquaintance who invited us (supposing us boyfriends) to dinner parties he considered tedious to the point of sobs, "Don't ever take me to one of those evenings again."

"One or another of those people might serve on an upper administrative tenure committee."

"If that's what you're going to become after you're tenured, you should run for the nearest exit"—at that point not exactly what I wanted to hear.

As it developed over time, Cal and I sharing an apartment resulted in a non-marriage definitely not made in heaven. It began to unravel through a series of confrontations such as housemates the world over would recognize all too well. He started by undermining the reputation of anybody I dated, "Oh, I ran into Jonas, that boy you brought home Monday night. He said his butt's still sore, and he's not sure he wants to keep the date you've made for Friday." That relationship washed down the drain as fast as suds in the sink. I, for my part, started to make fun of all the people Cal brought home, most of whom I found unattractive—and said so. "Where did you find him?" I asked about one of his tricks. "Even if he is dynamite in bed, which I doubt, you must need to turn the lights out before you do it." Comments like these would send Cal to the living room to flick his feather duster like a frenzied magic wand banishing evil spirits. He would then iron shirts furiously into the wee hours.

It became a matter of lasting out second semester, but not before a particularly painful incident in which, I'm ashamed to say, neither of us acted with any grace or dignity. Of course the conflict evolved from a dispute over a changeling child, with Cal cast as Titania and I as Oberon. What was that boy's name? Jared, or something like that? A handsomely tall, flighty blond undergraduate with pretensions to intellectual accomplishments, susceptible to almost anybody with some brains and a libido in overdrive. This description fit both me and Cal.

Cal had him first, and then lost interest, whereupon I asked him, "What, not homely enough?" Jared became drunk one night at a party, and he succumbed to me easily: I paralyzed him with a two minute kiss on the sofa and he followed me home. He insisted on missionary position exclusively (nothing else would do). This presented no hardship, given how much it aroused him: after he lowered his long, tan legs from my shoulders, the most gentle encouragement made him erupt as vehemently as Etna spewing lava. Cal saw him leaving in the morning and said, "Well, Thumper, you always content yourself with sloppy seconds." Or thirds, or fourths.

Cal, for spite, lured him back one night, "And jealous Oberon would have the child knight of his train to trace the forests wild; But Titania perforce withholds the loved boy, Crowns him with flowers and makes him all her joy . . . ." I should have retired quietly with some decorum. Instead I pounded on Cal's bedroom door, "Is Jared in there?" Cal opened the door and replied, "Well, you can have him next, just like you *always* do." The poor young man fled, naturally—in the altogether, carrying his clothes bunched to hide his tumescence—lost to both of us. Cal decided then and there to move out, which pleased me immensely.

"Go and move in with that hideously pocked little cracker, Barry!" I reacted without hesitation.

"This instant," he retorted. "I'll come back for my *accoutrement* when you're not here!"

For this unseemly exchange we later apologized to one another. We remained distant friends, cordial, not warm. By mutual agreement, we cancelled all benefits. The whole episode reminded me that I was, as you have plainly seen, difficult to live with. I guarded both my personal space and my privacy jealously. As a result of my misadventure with Cal, I became a keen student of other acquaintances' domestic arrangements, most of which filled me with trepidation.

5 *MÉNAGES ÉTRANGES*

The few gay faculty members who lived openly with others had made peculiar adjustments to domesticity in Pulpitville, so fraught was gay academic life for any amount of time in those parts. Some of these arrangements I found unattractive, some disgusting, and none produced a sane household existence.

The gay couple I came to know best consisted of an older academic in the psychology department and his somewhat more junior longtime companion. The larger community knew them as the Billy-Bobs, younger and older in that order. The students, less discriminating about age, regarded them simply as a pair of foolish old twanks (Cal's characterization when he asked not to attend yet another dinner party at their home). It's safe to say that however one regarded them, the Billy-Bobs brought bitter co-dependency to heights seldom rivaled and never surpassed.

Bob, the older and taller of the pair, had skin the texture and color of bread dough, receding hair, ample padding around his midriff, an upper-class Southern drawl, and a cleverly manipulative trick of thought. With his training in psychology, which he taught but didn't practice, he usually attempted to maneuver people into divulging some unsavory inner secret. He was somewhat pompous, cheated mildly at cards, and generally held forth as an expert on many things he knew little about. He had never left the state for more than two weeks, and therefore blended perfectly with the assertive provincialism of the academic institution for which he worked and with the naïve self-satisfaction of the community in which he lived.

Where Bob exuded fatuous self-confidence, Billy, the more diminutive of the duo, exhibited copious neurotic insecurities, replete with facial tic. His family had moved to Tennelina from Philadelphia during his childhood. Though he claimed a Southern pedigree, he could only make this assertion in the context of South Philly, for the accent had never quite deserted him. He bore faint traces of youthful beauty (with an accompanying infantile narcissism), but he dieted so severely to retain his boyish figure that he had shriveled into a hideously wizened dwarf. It became fairly clear that Bob controlled Billy by playing on his insecurities, while Billy used a history of former paramours to torment the perpetually jealous Bob.

The Billy-Bobs considered themselves the doyens of Pulpitville gay society, which led them to hold large cocktail parties with a lot of cheap liquor and elaborate dinner parties with some fairly bad food and mediocre wine. At dinner, for instance, they would serve mushy pasta that bled red sauce containing chunks of stringy mystery meat. Further courses included wilting salad and an almost flavorless dessert (the crème brûlée had the consistency of library paste—come to think of it, maybe it was). Andrew Ivanov sometimes accompanied me to these suppers and, knowing the difference between slop and haute cuisine, swore our hosts had obtained the ingredients at various food pantries around town. For the Billy-Bobs, though pretentious, were both cheap and avaricious.

Ménages Étranges

They had furnished their sprawling old home with items they "stored" for various friends who had moved out of town. As a result, none of the furniture had a particular style. The sofas exemplified nondescript post-war modernism, with sagging springs and worn out cushions. The colonial-style dining-room table had multiple rings left by glasses deposited at parties and not collected until the next day. And a number of the faux-Chippendale dining-room chairs diabolically featured collapsing backs or pieces that would fall off suddenly (though they looked safe at first), leading an apologetic guest to believe he had damaged something. If a friend passed away, the Billy-Bobs swooped in like vultures, offering comfort to the relatives and stripping anything they could out of the house ("Poor Henry wanted me to have that side table," Bob would drawl). Everything had the faint whiff of decay, rather as if Dorian Gray had disintegrated in public while the painting in his attic retrogressed toward youth. My favorite wall decoration in that house confirmed this impression. It had enjoyed an existence as a Japanese screen during some past era, but one couldn't quite tell, because the tempura and gold leaf used to decorate it had largely pealed away. Miss Havisham would have approved.

"Why do you put up with them?" Andrew asked me, moving to the heart of the matter, "They're tacky." The answer was simple: the superannuated Bob wielded influence by virtue of his seniority. He knew everybody on campus, resulting in dinner parties with guest lists composed incongruously of old-time colleagues (the sententious fossil quotient) and very young colleagues (the new-meat quotient), mixed to produce historical disquisitions, histrionic interactions, and an occasional under-the-table grope. A protective athletic cup came recommended for these affairs.

The main event at a Billy-Bob dinner party consisted of the inevitable skit performed by the hosts toward the end of the evening. Both drank to excess, but Bob, much larger and heavier, held it with more aplomb. When finally and truly plastered, he would begin to pontificate on everything from University politics (he knew where all the Pulpitville skeletons lay buried and gave accounts of the old days at excessive length) to national politics to music and art (about which he knew nothing). Billy, much more easily inebriated, would go along until his memory of events differed from Bob's (Billy had dropped out of the graduate program in English). An exchange might run:

(Bob in Southern drawl): "When Cornelius White presided over the University ('just after the Spanish-American War,' Andrew would mutter to me if he was present), he decided to combine (pronounced: 'combahn') the English and Drama Departments. And so President White called a meetin' of the assembled faculty to issue his decree, where'pon the chairs of those two departments took public exception to the notion."

(Billy in mildly clipped South Philly): "Bob that never happened! It was the other way around: White separated Drama from English."

"Sugar, do you want to tell this story?" Bob interrupted.

"Honey, if I did, I'd at least get it right."

"How would you know? I had this from a faculty member in the English Department," Bob insisted.

"Well, I studied in the English Department, so I should get the story straight," Billy whined, his face beginning to exhibit its pronounced involuntary twitch and his accent reverting even more noticeably to South Philly, "You never listen to anything I say."

"Darlin', I listen enough to know you're misreportin' events, for one thing. And for a second, you couldn't get anythin' 'straight' if you went through the ten years of the therapy you so desperately require. Anyhow, the President *must* have had those two departments combined, because how else except as an English graduate student could you have developed your *pro*clivity for drama?"

This last quip signaled informed guests to assume defensive positions. Would Billy lob his wine glass full of cheap red the length of the table at Bob (who had become fairly adept at dodging these missiles after 35 years of cohabitation)? Would he then ponce into the kitchen in a huff to prepare a flavorless dessert, knocking various items off the sideboard in his tipsy and petulant progress? Or would he stamp his foot like an enraged gnome and disappear, if not into thin air, then into his bedroom with a hearty slam of the door? The click of the lock gave Bob's cue to follow his partner and coax to no avail, "Sugar (sound of a falling objects,—a bookcase, bric-a-brac, perhaps a lamp), we have guests out here. Won't you come join the party?" (Possibly more falling objects or the sound of the bathroom door slamming.) Then Bob returned unremorseful and undeterred, "I'm sorry, he just gets this way, and there's nothin' to be done. Let's finish our supper." These semi-public altercations astonished first-time guests, they embarrassed occasional visitors, but they held a certain Grand Guignol amusement for war veterans such as Andrew and me.

Internecine strife reigned at all hours in the Billy-Bob household, in private just as in front of company. I once had a reason to call in the late morning without phoning ahead, only to behold a large damp splatter on one wall of the breakfast nook, the result of a badly aimed cup of coffee that had been allowed to drip slowly down the plaster. Billy explained, "He told me that nobody ever believes me. And I told *him* that he'd better believe me now!" We both paused to contemplate the graphic demonstration of this assertion. The Billy-Bobs alone could have kept one of the local establishments selling house paint in business. In future I tried assiduously not to arrive unannounced at their home on any account; I had no interest in watching the outbreak of World Wars III, IV, or V.

At the heart of their domestic friction lay the fact that Bob held a faculty position and Billy—unable to keep any job for very long because of his outbursts—took the role of faculty wife. Not only was this unusual for a gay couple (both men held jobs in the outside world, as a rule), but around this time women began to join the workforce in growing numbers. The Billy-Bobs' arrangement was already becoming passé in the

60s; in the early 80s it resembled nothing so much as a gay recasting of a 50s sitcom: *Leave It to Billy* or perhaps *Bob Knows Best*.

Billy's economic dependence increased not only his insecurity but also his resentment. He took this out in a series of affairs with, variously, a doctor, an orthodontist, a banker, and a lawyer, each liaison accompanied by repeated threats to leave Bob. But he never would. For one thing, nobody in their right mind would have put up with him for long. And for another, who else but phlegmatic Bob could serve as foil to Billy's overwrought neurasthenia? And so ructious day after ructious day, besotted night after besotted night, theatrical year after theatrical year, they toiled on. Repulsed by their continual bickering, I became increasingly attracted to Johannes Brahms's motto, "Single but Happy."

Another component of the Billy-Bob concordat entailed a perilous lack of judgement in renting basement rooms to a number of students (mostly graduate but occasionally undergraduate) selected for their looks, with a another mysterious renter in a semidetached apartment on the property. The students had kitchen privileges and circulated through the house and through parties. Bob was too old to carry on with them, but Billy would make an occasional pass or three, as he did with almost anybody else he could isolate in a secluded corner. Big cocktail parties—to which the Billy-Bobs would invite straight faculty acquaintances, neighbors, and gay friends—involved the basement residents as cater-waiters.

These large gatherings (with 200 extras in attendance) unfolded in two acts. Act I: the announced cocktail party from around 6-9 PM in which all the guests circulated between the various bars and among young men bearing plates of soggy hors d'oeuvres. Act II (the bachelor party): straight guests exited, gay guests remained. The resident students transformed from servers into objects of attention (or maybe servers of another kind), together with friends whom they would invite. I dreaded this phase. Drugs would appear, invariably pot, and also a certain amount of the uppers or downers of the day (cocaine and Quaaludes stood most in favor just then), supplied by Jim, the mystery tenant in the semidetached apartment. He had once belonged to a good-ol'-boy fraternity, and he made a living after his abysmal academic career by becoming Pulpitville's most enterprising and successful dope peddler. Now I try not to be censorious: what people do in private concerns them alone, unless they're axe murderers or child pornographers. But I disliked having students (some of them mine) present as people smoked joints, inhaled lines, and popped pills, especially since I didn't have tenure. Call me a prig, naïve, narrow-minded, or just plain self-protecting, as you will: drugged orgies didn't feature in my view of life in a small university town.

In Pulpitville, students and faculty inevitably mingled socially and had affairs (especially young faculty, so long as they honored the amorous First Commandment). The straight faculty dallied the most with the students because of the university's overwhelming heterosexuality. But I could avoid illegal activities, and the appearance of visiting a drug-infused gay boardinghouse seemed ill advised. When I made so bold as to caution Billy about this, he shrugged it off:

> Through all the Employments of Life
> Each Neighbor abuses his Brother;
> Whore and Rogue they call Husband and Wife:
> All Professions be-rogue one another:
> The Priest calls the Lawyer a Cheat,
> The Lawyer be-knaves the Divine:
> And the Scholar, because he's so great,
> Thinks his Trade as honest as mine.

The worst rogue in the gay household gallery was "Uncle Hank" Drury, a highly unattractive middle-aged faculty member in the School of Music. He lived on the upper floor of a house with its ground floor rented exclusively to attractive gay undergraduates, two to a room, making eight in all. This apparently eased his social isolation, for Hank had never dated anybody so far as anyone knew. And while he had little success with the downstairs harem (the boys could outrun him when he chased them around the house), they proved a draw for his summer pool parties. These he held in conjunction with two 30-something gay men who rented the house next door, which Hank also owned.

His summer festivals garnered fame throughout the immediate area and drew around 300 people, mostly the same people seen at gay discos, but without music drowning out all the conversation. Eventually the neighbors put a stop to these gatherings because of the parking problems they caused all along the narrow streets in the area. Residents finally summoned the police to clear the lanes. But for the several summers the pool parties endured, they enjoyed a certain cachet. They mixed all manner of gay men from a sixty-mile radius. And as such evenings progressed, when everybody became sufficiently drunk, members of the crowd would disappear into the forested landscaping around the property for sex or to the pool area for skinny-dipping entirely shielded from outside inspection by a high fence.

My presence at one of these events made me the subject of intense interest among Hank's downstairs lodgers the semester after Cal had decamped from my apartment. The cadre kept each other informed about eligible targets, and when I jumped into the pool buck naked one July night, a bright blip appeared on their radar. I had added allure, I later discovered, because I had been seen at a local eatery having dinner with a very pretty woman (a former graduate-school friend who wanted to visit Pulpitville). One of Hank's coterie bussed tables there, and he spread rumors of my heterosexuality around, thereby rendering me an even more desirable object of seduction. These fellows notched their bedposts and traded notes. So began a summer onslaught of undergraduate lovelies who provided another lesson about how I didn't want to live.

6 SUMMER BEAUTIES

Whoever wrote that "heaven is a banquet of twenty-year-olds" didn't come to know undergraduate men the way I did in Pulpitville during my third year there. I first learned from a siege of "Uncle Hank's boys," as outrageously deranged as they were attractive. Now you'd think I'd be grateful for the memory of lithe young bodies, comely features, physical endurance, and endless libidos. But their fleeting charm developed into a test of my sanity—the men in the cadre had already lost theirs. I don't know whether they drew straws for who would have first choice, but they must have plotted their sequential arrival. No sooner would I rid myself of one than another would appear. It proved mentally exhausting.

The assault began with young Brandon, freckled and much admired among students for his leadership of a male a-cappella group whose concerts were swarmed equally by female and male fans, perhaps for the same reason. Many in the chorus traded sex among themselves and with other men on campus. They also sampled some of the enthusiastic women.

Brandon had a healthy appetite for both sexes, though I think he must have tended towards men, because he partied at the local gay bar most weekends. That's where he pursued me the first night, chatting me up, sitting down with me on a banquette, and engaging in a thorough exploration of my dental work. It wasn't unpleasant, I must admit, but Brandon didn't desire just a cheap trick that evening. No, he wanted romance in the form of a dinner at my place, "I'll bring a bottle of red, you provide the steak" (and, he should have added, the beefsteak). He had a youthful figure, not particularly developed, but slim and pleasant.

Brandon had no car, so I picked him up at Uncle Hank's, where he waited on the curb holding the promised bottle. I made cocktails, grilled a couple of steaks, and we proceeded to divide the wine between us, which went much more to his head than to mine. He had a capital idea for dessert: hot popsicle. This involved his submersion under the table and reemergence at my lap, where he swiftly and expertly undid my zipper, drew the confection he sought out of my shorts, and proceeded to use his well-practiced lips. He stopped for a moment to say, "Please don't come in my mouth," to which I replied, "Then you'd better slow down." He looked up at me, smiled sweetly, and moved me into the bedroom, where I returned his interest in dessert. But he really wanted something his girlfriends couldn't provide (unless they used dildos on their dates): a massage of his prostate (I came with batteries included), while he rubbed himself down (and off). He spent the night, and I kept drilling him at intervals until he pleaded with me, "I don't think I can take it any longer."

We repeated pretty much the same ritual on three more evenings in two weeks, until we mutually lost interest. He was almost entirely passive in bed, and I grew a little bored. He stopped chatting me up at the bar and stopped calling me at home, which suited me fine. Yesterday's kisses are bygone, thank heaven. I thought this would end the stream of Hank's boys.

No sooner had Brandon and I disengaged, however, than I received a call from Mark, one of his fellows at Hank's Sanitarium for Gay Undergraduates. Mark was an especially virile bisexual young man who had come to Pulpitville from a well known New-England prep school. He never appeared at the gay bars, but he had taken a class with me two years before. He used his constantly shop-bound European car as an excuse for missing exams, resulting in follow-up visits to my office. He'd come to do postmortems of the make-up test, and during the first such embassy he let it be known that he had a room at Hank Drury's place. "Do you know him?" he inquired leadingly. "Yes," I replied, changing the subject hastily, "Now about your exam."

Mark was highly intelligent and also sufficiently perceptive to figure out my sexual tendencies long before they became a topic of interest among his fellow travelers at Hank's. As I sat looking at one of his exams, he knelt by my side, rubbing his beautifully furred arm over mine as he asked me to decipher various comments I had made. I confess that I found it difficult not to make a pass, but I resisted somehow while he was still a student in my class.

Two years later, during the summer parade of lovelies, I couldn't hold back any longer. I frequented a local restaurant where Mark worked at as a waiter to pay his summer bills, and he would stop by my table to chat. One night he deliberately bumped my chair, and I asked whether I had injured him, thinking it was my fault. "Oh, nothing you couldn't soothe with a massage," he replied and called the next day to make an appointment for his physical therapy. "When are you free?" I inquired obligingly.

"How about this afternoon?"

What anticipation I had about this apparently nubile, chocolate-haired, prep-school lovely on whom I already had a crush. He must, have learned, I imagined, more sophisticated and novel techniques from his boarding-school dorm mates than I could possibly dream. Not exactly. He showed up fetching and ready, stripping to reveal a lightly furred chest and sturdy equipment already semi-engorged. He embraced and kissed passionately, then offered his sizeable endowment for fondling and massage, but nothing more. I had regressed to junior high. He remained tremendously stiff while I stroked him methodically until he launched, and he returned the massage as a favor. I wanted to ask, *That's it? No chomping on the kielbasa, no sampling the clam sauce, no making like a squirrel and eating nuts, no porking?*

Maybe we could work up to more varied pursuits in stages. During our next afternoon session (he dated women at night when he wasn't waiting table) we progressed to licking each other, though I can't say he had much talent for that. The next afternoon I combined this with fingering his tightly puckered sphincter, which he permitted without enthusiasm, though he liked it more when he was doing it to me. This should have been a clue, but I didn't take the hint. I finally thought I had worked up to the main event of reaming his brains out.

"Wait! Nick, stop," he objected when I threw his legs over my shoulders. His eyes grew very large, and as I desisted, panting, he explained, "In the first place, that's too much to handle. And in the second place, if anybody does that, I'm the one."

Ah, the classic dilemma. We were both pitchers. I was never going to slide into his warm, sweet, smooth interior, and so we agreed to cease our afternoon liaisons. My fantasies went unrealized, and in the last analysis I hadn't gone any further with Mark than with Wes in high school. *No more Hank boys*, I thought.

But the campaign had not ended by a long shot. Upon Mark's departure, the third wave of the invasion, rolled in using a transparent but novel gambit, "Hi, this is Terry Johnson—is this Professor Walker? You don't know me, but I live over at Hank's. I wonder whether I could speak with Cal Blount. I'd like to have dinner with him."

"Sorry, Cal and I don't share a place anymore, and I don't have his new number."

"Oh, I see," he continued undeterred, "Well, how about you. Would you go out with me?"

What was I? One of the selections in a box of bonbons: if somebody has eaten the one you want, you settle for another? Of course, knowing that Mark had left the picture, Terry had his license to hunt. And of all the summer parade he held by far the most attraction. He had film-star good looks, broad shoulders, a muscular chest, and a very winning smile that seemed to promise clean-cut innocence, rather like a beach-movie heartthrob. His only revealing flaw when I first became aware of him around Pulpitville lay in his habit of changing hair color. He was a natural dirty blond that paired well with his blue eyes. But he would sometimes change the color to dark brown, which made him look like a different person, but for the beauty spot on his left cheek. Either way, he was still gorgeous: who wouldn't want to go out with him and do a good deal more afterwards? I caved instantly to dinner and a movie, and I suggested he come over beforehand for a drink.

Terry offered high-class merchandise, and I bought a bottle of champagne to let him know what a prize I thought him (every gay man in town wanted a date). He came straight from working out, dressed in tight-fitting jeans and a white button-down shirt. I suggested a drink on my back patio, but on that very warm evening he preferred sitting, air-conditioned, inside. When I cracked the bottle of champagne he expressed suitable appreciation, and the sparkling wine went immediately to his head (and to other areas). He started kissing me and then sticking his hand into the pocket of my pants to find what he expected. I almost wanted to hit the bed then, but we had little time for the dinner and the movie, so we shoved off. He seemed a really wholesome, well-adjusted fellow, he laughed a lot, and he made good company.

We returned to my place for what I hoped would be the grand finale, necked some more on the sofa, and then he asked, "Strip me, man."

"Do you want slow or fast?"

"Oh, let's make it slow. I want it to last."

Anything your heart desires, I thought. He stood completely still as I unbuttoned his shirt to reveal some terrific nipples that I licked in leisurely fashion. Then I loosened his jeans, pulled off his socks, and slid the jeans down to reveal his boxers. He didn't appear to be aroused, but he was, I discovered to my surprise. When I slowly pulled down his shorts, his diminutive member emerged, like something one would find on the statue of a Baroque Eros, an appropriate deity at least.

He looked down, a little embarrassed, "Hope you weren't expecting much."

"I like everything I see." I'm always amazed to see a large fellow with tiny equipment. It's rather cute.

"Do you have any belts or rope?"

"For what?"

"Sir, I want you to tie me up. I've been so bad, I need to be punished, sir."

Now this was new, and I said, "Sure, just a second," and went to retrieve some webbed nylon belts I had stashed in my dresser.

"Sir, tie my hands behind my back and wrap that other belt around my ankles, tight!" He submitted, unresisting, while I immobilized him in a kneeling position.

"Okay," after I had finished, "What now?"

"Strip." I wasn't slow and I popped out ready for action.

"Fuck my mouth, sir—hard, fast, and deep."

With pleasure, I thought. But when I started to launch, I pulled away, wanting to prolong, "Not yet!"

"Then, sir, please whip me, sir"

"Oh?"

"With that belt, on my butt. Then fuck me!"

I really didn't want to hurt the fellow, but he kept asking for more lashes. After about two more strokes he sprayed all over the carpet, my legs, and the nearby furniture, no hands, with an expression of surprised gratification. Terry had a hairpin trigger, and after he fired, he became impatient to depart:

> Wilt thou unkind thus reave me
> Of my heart, and leave me?
> Farewell! But yet or e're you part, O Cruel,
> Kiss me sweet, my jewel.

Because he provided such good company and good looks, we had a couple more outings along these lines before I realized that I would never score a home run. He threw too quickly for me to slide into the plate. *No more Hank boys,* right? No such luck. The fourth assault wave outdid the previous three.

He went by the name of Kevin, and while he certainly had nice looks, his main attraction lay in a spectacular body constantly on display at the disco, stripped to the waste every evening. He wasn't just cut, he was chiseled, a gym addict extraordinaire. And he really went for faculty members, especially ones he thought might be straight, because he was the one who saw me having dinner with a female acquaintance that fateful night. Rumor had it that Kevin liked brief tête-à-têtes—each party kneeling for the right kind of head—in the parking lot of the disco after dancing. I had participated discretely in such exercises on occasion, and I thought little more about it. I didn't know he liked to go "buck naked" for these outdoor encounters.

As soon as Terry had left the picture Kevin called, and against my better judgment, I invited him to lunch. He proved a nervous young man, lacking in self-confidence, rather like Billy (of the Billy-Bobs) at a younger age. Lord knows, though, the boy had a voracious appetite for sex. A couple of drinks at lunch, and he chomped at the bit, so to speak. I barely escorted him through the door of my place when he attacked me, tearing off my clothes and his, going down on me in a most expert way and then proceeding to offer himself for the same treatment, which I gave gladly. He liked to moan and plead, "Oh, Nick, so goooood, man, keep going, keep going, so goooood," until he had reached the finish line. Oral only for Kevin; he had a shallow throat, and he told me he didn't like rear entry, "Even if I could take you, which I doubt." But I couldn't resist such a beautiful body, and I accepted whatever terms he offered.

This began a series of dates that became increasingly unreal. He'd call, come over for dinner, and suggest penne with clam sauce (his and mine) for hors d'oeuvres. He'd announce, as he walked in the door, "I'm not wearing any underwear." This called for cocktails, some wrestling on the floor, and then sex in the living room, in the kitchen, in the bedroom, in the shower—anyplace the spirit moved him, always following the same routine. I wasn't bored: just licking his washboard stomach gratified in itself. What fun!

Then came the night for a more involved date— dinner and a movie. He chose *Flash Gordon*, starring Sam Jones stripped half naked in various poses suggestive of S & M. Jones had appeared in *Playgirl*, a favorite rag with gay men, and the movie he starred in came as close to soft-core porn as one could find in Pulpitville. Dinner that night did not follow its usual course. Kevin came without undergarments, true, but served no penne before the main course. In our conversation over supper he said mischievously, "I bet Terry would like to see this one with you. We used to share a bedroom at Uncle Hank's."

"How was that?" I inquired out of curiosity.

"We don't like each other at all. I mean, nice pecs, but his abs need some work. And that little dick. What'd you guys do?"

"Why don't you ask him," I responded.

"I don't think he'd tell me. But I tell him all about us. I think he's jealous," Kevin teased. So that was the game. I represented a trophy date. I wondered idly whether they kept a scoreboard at Uncle Hank's, with columns for various faculty conquests, listing the players (Brandon, Mark, Terry, Kevin), a tally of singles, doubles, triples, and home runs, (my batting average was 1000, but only 4 runs in my stats, all with Brandon, the only one to let me slide into home base). I abandoned this reverie as Kevin enticed me until I became very excited, and then said, "Let's go to the show" (no dessert either, alas).

He bought the tickets, making sure we sat toward the back of the theater. And as Kevin watched Jones in various alluring poses, he snuck his hand up my khaki shorts to massage me (it didn't take much to start inflating), and I moved my hand up his shorts to fondle him (he had become stiff too). One young man, fairly attractive, sat right behind us, but I don't think he noticed anything. Kevin leaned his head over, as if to make a comment, whispering, "Wouldn't it be cool if I went down on you right here? Do you think the guy behind us would join in?"

Danger, Nick Walker, Danger! I invited Kevin to a restroom conference, "I need to visit the facility. Why don't you come along." With nobody else inside, luckily, I whispered, "Are you out of your everloving mind? Do you know what an arrest on a morals charge would look like? They'd expel you and fire me. If you want that, let's go home." So we left and drove home.

When we arrived back, we sat down on the sofa and Kevin asked for a glass of water. Then, "You don't need to get all huffy about it."

"Look, sorry about that. But this is a small town, and one arrest is going to travel the circles of gossip, gay and straight, forever. So don't pull that stunt again."

Kevin began foreplay meant only to frustrate me. He was angry that I hadn't gone along with his movie-theater exhibitionism, and he wanted to torment me just a little on that account. In fumbling around, he knocked over the glass of water on a table, spilling it across the living room. I threw him out, hoping that a general report would reach the cadre.

The phone calls stopped, and no other undergraduates who sauntered through my classes asked whether I knew Hank Drury as a prelude to requesting some special treatment. I played dumb even at the mention of Uncle Hank's name and avoided his parties, acquaintances, and boys.

But Pulpitville moved in small circles, and I had to run the gauntlet with Andrew, "So, I hear you've been dating Tennelina cuties from the Hank stable."

"Say again—I don't know what you're talking about," I replied disingenuously.

"Do you think those boys kiss and *don't* tell? Every gay man in this town knows about it," came the immediate retort, "And it's useless to play innocent with me. By the way, you look a little worn out. Maybe some wrinkle cream or a little rest would help?"

"My, aren't we in fine form today. Jealous?"

"Of course—they're all cute. And they're as crazy as bedbugs. I'd check for crabs, and I don't mean softshell. Oh, by the way, everybody knows that Kevin's a lunatic exhibitionist from his virtuoso performances in public."

"My illustrious friend and joy of my liver, have I ever explained that envy ill becomes you? I realized my mistake too late. And since when have you given advice so freely?"

"Have I ever explained that very good looking people wear sarcasm badly? And who but your gay best friend would tell you the ugly truth?" he gloated.

Of course I owned up to my activities, and then related to Andrew the last episode, which didn't particularly surprise him. You might think I'd have learned my lesson. But life afforded me one more chance to edify myself at the heavenly banquet of twenty-year-olds, much to Andrew's amusement.

7 FALL TEAMS

The next undergraduate shoals and reefs lay just below the waterline, so to speak, during my fifth semester, in the form of the lacrosse team, which shared the same locker room as junior faculty. One afternoon they concluded their practice at the same time I finished working out, and showering with those rambunctious young men made for exquisite torture. One of their number, the brunette, well-built Matt, sat on the floor with his back resting on one of the tiled walls while his teammates and I showered, his eyes level with our equipment. Most of the men on the team came from elite private boarding schools, instate or out, and they shared ample experience with what one might call male-on-male bonding. In any event, lacrosse players have a very wild streak engrained. Matt's buddies had a clear idea what he sought (it turned out later another of his teammates followed his train of thought precisely). And I couldn't conceal my interest (which became semi-evident in the showers).

The weekend after this initial inspection and appraisal, Matt and I happened to work out at the same time on a Sunday. With the locker room entirely deserted, he joined me in sluicing off, looked over, and then entreated, "Could you wash my back where I can't reach?"

"Ah, . . . sure," I answered, meaning, *I'll help you with anything you want any time you want.* I started with at his shoulder blades and moved slowly downward, stopping gently in the small of his back. I paused, wondering how far the invitation extended.

"How about you?" he inquired without hesitation. He returned the favor and then some, standing behind me and soaping me from my back downward and then reaching around front, where he found exactly what he hoped to discover. This led to further practice with balls and sticks (lacrosse is a contact sport, after all) until we had both scored. I thought this would end our practice, but when we toweled off, he asked me for my phone number, which I provided readily.

"I'll give you a call if I have some time next weekend," he offered rather shyly.

He didn't wait long to call, on Tuesday in fact, "Hey, this is Matt, from the gym?" (You're right: I hadn't remotely forgotten.) "So, what're you doin' Friday night later, say around 11?"

In your case I'm available at any and all hours, I thought, but I answered, "I'll be around." He probably had a date early in the evening or a party to attend, and I had planned to go out to the disco. That agenda changed right then and there. I called Andrew, "I can't go out Friday. Sorry."

"Who is he?"

"Nobody you would know."

"I know lots of men. Give me a try."

"Trust me, he's a novice."

"Out abducting the local virgins, if there be any, *tovarich*?"

"Look, I'll explain later."

"You will, or no more cooking for you."

"Promise I'll tell all at some point. Now call off the Cossacks."

Matt appeared around the appointed time, and he looked adorable, not just because of his rugged jock features, but because he had scrubbed up for the occasion in true prep-school style: he wore khakis and a button-down shirt, loafers without socks, and he had applied a liberal dose of cologne—all over I soon discovered. I wonder if he had considered bringing flowers. He was out to score, a little nervous, and he wanted to be well received. He knocked quietly on the door and stood fidgeting, "Professor Walker?"

I invited him in, "Call me Nick. We might not have been formally introduced, but we've gotten to know one another just a little bit."

"Yes sir."

"And you don't need to call me 'sir'."

"Yes sir," came the anxious reply.

Matt wanted guidance. We hadn't kissed in the locker-room showers or done much more than massage. But after I retrieved a drink for him, Matt immediate wanted to neck on the sofa. It was refreshing, after the Uncle-Hank crazies, to meet this reticent and polite young man. He didn't know exactly how two men proceeded, and he wondered about what was required to win the trophy. And what was the trophy, anyhow? True to the faults of their gender, gay men don't like to stop and ask directions. (Oh, and you out there: don't you recall when you knew in theory how all the equipment worked but you'd never played a practice game, tossed the ball around a bit with other players instead of by yourself? Don't deny it—you can't fool me.) In this case, I thought it wise to inquire of the aspiring learner, "So, what do you imagine you'd like to do?"

"Well, I'm not really sure. I mean, I've never done anything with a guy or anybody until we hit the showers last weekend," he offered, a little ashamed that he had practically no experience at all, save for flying solo.

"I see," trying not to sound too surprised, though the evident embarrassment made him even more endearing.

He flushed a little, "Sorry."

"Nothing to apologize for," I reassured. "Do you have any fantasies?"

"Let's get naked."

A solid beginning, but clearly I would need to walk him through this. I began unbuttoning his shirt (we had already seen each other in the buff, so there couldn't be any surprises). Then I moved down kissing him until I reached the soft hair around his nipples, which I tongued and nibbled very lightly. He whimpered. All the while I had my hand on his thigh and moved it up slowly. Matt learned quickly and reversed roles to do the same for me, but he went a little further, undoing my belt and loosening the waistband of my pants. We explored for signs of arousal. Yes, we had our sticks ready for play to begin.

"Let's go into the bedroom," I suggested.

"Yeah, let's." By this time he was breathless with excitement, but when I shed all my clothes he registered surprise, "What's that?"

"A ring to hold an erection longer—also it feels great. Try one? I've a lot of them, although it's harder to put on when you're, well, up for it." We both looked at his engorged stick. "But some lube will help slip it on." He liked the gliding feel of my hand on his balls.

And then another significant question, "Do you shave your nuts, man?"

"Yes. A little trim makes everything smooth."

"Show me how." A teacher imparts experience one can't always find in books. Shaving him (very carefully) drove him almost crazy. And thus prepared, we "fed" each other (to borrow a lacrosse term) and "cradled" balls for a while, until we just couldn't wait any longer to drink a liquid reward.

After it was over, he asked to stay the night, and I had no aversion to that. He seemed very like an affectionate puppy, though a big one. When he left early the following morning for the dorm, he asked tentatively, "Next weekend, maybe Saturday?"

"Works for me!"

Matt arrived right on cue the following Saturday, same outfit, same cologne. And after the basic routine (except that he had learned to shave himself), he wanted to know more, "Like, man, do you ever insert that d-pole of yours into guys?"

"D-pole?"

"Ah, the long stick in lacrosse." The Hallelujah Chorus, sung by three hundred voices accompanied by full symphony orchestra, sounded somewhere in the background.

"It's my favorite thing. But I must warn you, it can hurt at first. Do you want to try?"

"Yeah, lots of lube."

"Sure, and maybe some of this," I held up a bottle.

"What's that?"

"'Poppers' in the vernacular. They give a rush and they can also relax you." He took a big sniff, rolled over on his side, and pleaded, "Okay, man. Slow."

Once he was comfortable, he really liked this kind of practice. He slept over again, and that allowed a couple more sessions during the night.

"Next weekend?"

"Which night?"

"Don't know whether on Friday or Saturday. Call you later next week?"

"Sure."

Andrew finally had to know something, "Okay, confess. What's up. You didn't go out on Friday, and now you're busy Saturday. Who?"

"An athlete. And that's all your getting for now."

"You aren't working your way through the football team? I've heard about them."

"Close, but no brass ring, so to speak. If you're a very good boy, you'll hear eventually."

"If *you're* a very good boy, I'll cook a *poulet sauté à la creme* for you," he snickered

"I'll let you know if I'm in the mood for chicken."

"True, it might be redundant: sounds like you're already eating plenty, with cream to boot."

I shot him a dirty look, "The fellow is at least twenty. And don't pretend you're innocent on that score."

"As often as I can," he replied smugly.

Matt called dutifully on Thursday, "Hi, still up for something this weekend?"

"Why not?"

"Well, I have a favor to ask . . . ."

"Being?"

"I wanna bring my friend Daniel. You saw him in the shower, the guy with the short-cut, reddish-brown hair. We . . . ." He was beginning to lose his nerve and spoke very apologetically, "We attended prep school together, and I told him where I spent last Saturday night. He asked to come along."

Any caution gave way to a fantasy of them arriving at my front door, "Hey coach, how's it going. Ready for a scrimmage? Where're the poppers and lube?" This vision didn't prove too inaccurate in the event.

"If you really don't like the idea," Matt became very unsure, "then he doesn't need to tag along. I mean, I know it's a lot to ask, . . . but I want him to meet you. And he already knows kinda who you are, 'cause he noticed you in the showers, and I told him about last week and the first time, I mean, like . . . ." This came out in a rush of sincere confession, so anxiously that I couldn't turn him down. (All right, you know I drooled because Daniel had the most striking looks and beautiful body of any man on the lacrosse team. His reddish brown fury chest had a matching track that ran down to the grove between his muscular legs. A sweet mischievous smile completed his beauty. And who doesn't fantasize about threesomes?)

"Okay, but you two need to behave yourselves. No craziness, no drugs."

"Yes sir." How could I refuse such a dutiful young man?

They arrived identically clad, wearing the same cologne (I think they would have worn school blazers and ties if I had asked them), bringing with them a pint of gin as a present (Matt knew I liked martinis).

"Come in, gentlemen."

Daniel, okay Dan, didn't exhibit Matt's shyness at all, and he had also asked his buddy for some pointers. After a preliminary drink we moved right away to the bedroom and stripped off fast. Dan had shaved in preparation (they learned quickly from each other, these fellows), and I made the gift of another ring, which seems to have become an initiation rite for the team. After some preliminary fluffing, one on one, two on one, various combinations, I asked, "So what would you like to do. I mean, I know what Matt likes."

Dan had a good idea of how he wanted to start, "I wanna watch you pump him."

A polite host caters to the desires and pleasures of his guests, "Well, if you want to watch, then maybe Matt should control the proceedings." I lay on the bed, completely ready, and told Matt, "Now, climb on and sit down just as slowly as you want, as long as it feels good." When we were really set, with Matt riding on top of me, he fed Dan his luscious stick. Matt loved it, and he whimpered until he finally said, "Dan, I'm really near. Do you want it?" Dan certainly did, and after gagging a little, he swallowed every last drop. I finished too, and out of breath, Matt and I collapsed on each other. Dan kneeled above us, unsatisfied.

"Could we give Dan a little help? I mean, he's the only one hasn't gotten off," Matt pleaded. More than prepared to aid the needy, Matt and I proceeded to double team a very grateful young man. Dan had never sampled poppers either, and he too whimpered until he exploded massively in our mouths. I noticed for the first time consciously around these athletes how much sex between men resembled a team effort. We all helped each other to the goal and then collapsed in celebration of sweet victory.

We hit the showers and rested for about 45 minutes. Then Dan implored, "Could you do the thing to me you just did to Matt?" Lacrosse has four fifteen minute periods, after all.

"Sure. Why not?"

"Okay, Dan. . . . Has Matt warned you about handling the stick deftly until you're comfortable? You need to tell me how fast to go and whether you're enjoying it," I advised.

His eyes grew very wide, "Yeah, ah, where're are the lube and poppers." I repeated the drill, this time on Dan with his legs on my shoulders and Matt's head buried in Dan's lap to help him reach the goal. Then we both helped Matt score. We began to generate that wonderful scent of men exerting themselves in athletic contests, cologne mingled with the aroma of sweat and testosterone. We needed half-time entertainment:

> Strive with the team on the field,
> Show them Tennelina's here,
> Set the bed reverberating with a mighty cheer.
> Yeah! Yeah! Yeah!
> Ream them hard, see how they fall,
> Never let them cease to ball,
> Hail, hail, the gangs all here,
> So thump them 'til they come!

The third quarter an hour later featured a different playbook, Matt in Dan and then Dan in Matt, both them feeding me with their sticks. You must run all the plays if you want to memorize them, and so they double-teamed me at the end.

Would there be rest for the weary? Absolutely not. We had dozed for another hour when they awakened me, grinning, ready for the last quarter. Dan asked boldly, "So, Nick. Would you let me try it on you? . . . . I mean in you?" I was really sensitive in that area and hesitated. Dan, however, appeared by far the easiest to accommodate of the two. Turnabout seemed fair play, and I had to take one for the team.

"Okay, but please, go really, really slow."

He slid into me so gently—"Am I hurting you, man? Just tell me to stop, if I am," he leaned forward to kiss me to ease any discomfort—that I really enjoyed it. And I fed Matt's soft lips and tongue until we achieved a goal that ached for a minute. I thought I'd die ("with thee again in sweetest sympathy"). Then Matt had to feed me and Dan, lest he should go without scoring for that quarter. Thank God the teammates finally fell soundly asleep, everybody entwined in everybody else's luscious salt aroma. Before they left the next morning, my charges insisted on helping me put the sheets we had soiled in the wash and make the bed up fresh. Then they departed as politely and gratefully as they had arrived, with a small kiss and a shy smile.

I don't think I could have repeated that night: it left me a physical wreck. And the duo didn't ever call for a return match. But I saw them for the rest of their time in college, always in each other's company. They started going to my church, they remained sociable, like athletes who had battled on the same field, and after they graduated, they both went off to the same law school. It seemed fairly clear that they wanted some pointers on how to start, but that they had actually fallen in love with each other. I hope that terrific pair still plays together. Though our time spent in bed fulfilled my fantasy superbly, they left me feeling more avuncular than romantic, a little like Friar Lawrence, "Therefore love moderately; long love doth so; Too swift arrives as tardy is too slow." The next year the athletic department found new quarters for the lacrosse team, affording the athletes their own locker room and me some peace of mind.

When I finally related all of this to Andrew, his first incredulous reaction ran, "At the same time? How very immoderate!" followed by a snide, "Well, maybe some of the other teams are available. Or you could advertise private tutoring for athletes."

"Thanks. Put it in the suggestion box. But I'll take a pass for now. I used to be twenty at one time—you may have been too, a long time ago—but I don't think I can survive the practices any more. And by the way, you haven't forgotten that you owe me dinner."

"Maybe we should consider something vegetarian?" he mused. "You seem to have had enough protein—not to mention meat—for the rest of the term."

"You think you're funny, don't you, Prince Mishkin. Do you remember your comment about sarcasm from good looking men."

"That sounds like flattery, which you need to lay on with a trowel in the case of royalty. That's Prince Ivanov to you, lowly pheasant, and I *am* clever and funny."

Andrew split the difference between meat and poultry, preparing an exquisite *filets de poisson gratinés, à la Parisienne* and a risotto, with *service à la Russe*, of course.

Faculty also receive an education at a university. Attraction to the beauty of twenty-year-olds comes unavoidably. But they aren't heaven (and I was no saint), just hungry, inquisitive, and naïve. I learned about their intense neediness, their perplexed indecision, and their endearing desire to learn from an older man (I recalled when nineteen seemed "mature" to me). Moreover, there's a comradeship that develops when one has even casual sex with another man, a kind of love that comes from having collaborated on the work at hand. But I needed to pursue my quest for deeper and more lasting affection elsewhere, among a more adult and stable cohort, if I could discover one.

8 STYLISTS AND FLORISTS AND CLERKS, OH MY!

If you've been paying attention at all to this point—you have been paying attention, haven't you?—you may have reached the not entirely unjustifiable conclusion that I was a spoiled, snobbish, self-centered, callow sex-addict with one thing on his mind: whom I might bed next. Have just a little charity, please! I'd wager you were 29 once too. How does the generalization run: a man thinks about sex every ten seconds? In my case it might have been every five or just plain continual obsession. So let me beg your pardon at this point for the portraits I'm about to paint ("For these and all other sins which I cannot now remember I humbly repent"—more or less). After all, a group of likeminded men engaged with me in my pursuits. But they don't have the opportunity to defend themselves against my characterization of their failings. If I dwell on the latter, a disclaimer: in my experience everybody is fundamentally deranged (that includes you), some benignly so, some perniciously. I might define affection, friendship, or love as the ability to overlook or even come to appreciate another fellow's peccadilloes. None of these ravenous lovers worked out in the end, perhaps on account of my lunacy, perhaps on account of theirs. It always takes two.

My first seriously adult affair unfolded with Keith Sherer, a local pharmacist. He too found himself in his late 20s, quite tall, sandy-haired, sweet, and vaguely unreliable, at least as a boyfriend. He sported a self-effacing smile, a Southern drawl, and a python in his pants that scared me to death. We dated off and on for years (when I had no other boyfriend, he would attempt to fill the void). But we started with a steady six months of going to the movies, attending church, dinners out, and assorted extracurricular activities. We had absolutely nothing in common, and I had no idea what to do with his incredible endowment. We both preferred to pitch and therefore suited each other poorly. We tried mightily, however, to think why we should continue to see each other. Perhaps we just sought company and somebody to cuddle at night. Or perhaps we both entertained the thought that we should look earnestly for what Keith called DKM: definite kinship material.

Keith had a lot going for him in the kinship department. He exhibited intelligence, a good sense of humor, a reticence to play the Southern card (he maintained no illusions about coming from the plantation aristocracy), and he made good conversation at dinner parties. The test for the latter came in an evening with the Billy-Bobs, to whom Keith reacted with cool aplomb.

Our dating nevertheless became less and less frequent. I circled warily around Keith in bed, and in his kindness he could not bring himself to prescribe the sigmoidoscopy for me that he could certainly have administered. "Cruel fate! Tyrannical Eros. Is this how you rewarded him for his devotion"—by providing an opener without a can? He finally broke up our steady relationship with a memorable gesture. He came late to a party for my thirtieth birthday, stayed until all the other guests had left (I assumed he would provide the cherry for my cake), presented me with a very expensive Pendleton wool blanket, and told me he didn't want to see me regularly any more. I can't say I felt devastated, and I kept the blanket as a souvenir of our time together and for warmth on cold winter nights. I named it the Keith Scherer Memorial Blanket. It has lasted forever, a tribute to its quality if not to undying affection. "It's like bumper cars," Andrew explained, "You just keep running into one another (or did he say 'bumping one another'?) until you hit the right one." *C'est la vie.*

For the remainder of my time in Pulpitville Keith would call very occasionally to arrange dinner when he had nobody in prospect, and we carried on in a desultory way. We basically liked each other, but made no extended plans. Every so often I'd materialize on his front porch to claim *droit du seigneur* after a failed night at the bars, though this didn't always prove opportune. Which brings me to my next serious prospect, Stephen Sizemore, a Protestant seminarian with a void to be filled.

Stephen picked me up at the bar, as Keith had, and took me home. Between the sheets we were roughly compatible. Stephen, as an aggressive bottom, lived in thrall to ample men, and I had at least something to offer (though not quite enough, you'll see). He could exhaust me, since he never tired of catching, and I couldn't pitch for eighteen innings. Eventually one can't throw strikes anymore. I introduced Stephen around to my friends, who disapproved (and told me so categorically). "That man is trouble," Andrew advised. "He'll be ordained, marry some unsuspecting woman, and leave town for his first congregation. He's also sly and twisted à la Leather Minister" (remember him?). Our dating missed more than it hit.

Concluding that Stephen was not for me, I reverted to the search. And between boyfriends, I showed up one night a little drunk on Keith's doorstep. He had somebody with him that night, and I slept on the sofa. When I awakened in the morning, Keith snuck out of his bedroom to explain that I needed to leave, but not before I saw Stephen's naked recumbent form face down on Keith's bed. The perfect fit: Keith had the extraordinary length, depth and breadth that could fill Stephen completely. It injured my ego just slightly to think of them together, but I couldn't compete with Keith's extraordinary fire hose. Good merchandise finds a ready buyer. This episode came as the inevitable result of the constricted orbits through which we all rotated.

My two former boyfriends carried on regularly until Stephen was ordained, dutifully married, and assigned to a congregation in Maryland. Even then he gave up Keith's immense talent reluctantly. But here Keith demurred: "Do you know what he wants me to do?" he related during one of our rare later trysts. "He wants me to visit him and his wife in Maryland and sleep with him when he can sneak out. I told him no." Keith had a good heart, and this didn't fit his moral canon, no matter whatever else he fit. No other prospective pharmacists or clergymen presented themselves.

The next batters in the lineup formed a pair only because they were similarly attractive, kind, intelligent, and entirely inappropriate, each in his own way. One could have cast Jason and Rolland quite plausibly as brothers, both with naturally curly, naturally blond hair (you don't really need to ask how I verified the latter, do you?), terrific figures, amazing blue eyes, and wonderful bedside manners. Both worked in hair salons, where their female clients rightly adored them for their gentle attentiveness. Both made the rounds of the bars in the vicinity of Pulpitville, where they had grown up. Both particularly liked college professors. What could possibly go wrong?

If I have any regrets about my dating, they stem from the affair with Jason King. He was tall, slender, almost completely smooth, and totally smitten with me (he liked men with dark features). I met him at a disco in the neighboring town, where he lived. And from the first night he took me home he was solicitous. Sleeping with him held much allure, as did awakening with him: he'd slip downstairs to prepare an elaborate breakfast (waffles or pancakes, bacon or sausage, scrambled eggs sometimes, hot coffee) and then make inventive suggestions about what we might do for the rest of the day.

Since we worked in two different towns, we only spent weekends together, and he devised a whole series of outings in the area. We would hike through the local forests, bike around the neighborhoods, go to the movies, go dancing, or just spend Saturday evening with a bowl of popcorn in front of the TV. Because he knew I liked classical music, he made a special effort to acquaint himself with that genre. People often remember dating by the pieces of music playing when they meet, when they spend time with each other, when they travel together. And I associate Jason with his love of Rachmaninoff's *Rhapsody on a Theme by Paganini.*

The piece has a very lyrical section that served as a love theme in the movie *Somewhere in Time* when we were dating. I lacked the physical bulk to equal Christopher Reeve's (the male lead in the film), but Jason touchingly thought of me that way.

The domestic compatibility, the good sex (Jason agreed to almost anything and did everything well), the relaxing weekends all spoke in his favor. I especially liked my hair appointments with him, which he arranged at the end of his day at the salon, when everybody had left. He'd lock the door of the shop and put up the "closed" sign, then begin to cut my hair. Standing very close to me as he worked, the fly of his pants would brush my elbow under the smock I was wearing. I'd eventually sneak my hand out from under the folds of cloth, unzip him, and he'd pop out for a massage. After he had finished with my hair, he'd zip up and take me back to the shampoo area where he'd strip and bend over the sink to receive an extra tip. Other times he'd take the smock off after my haircut and unzip me to give extra service while I tipped back in the chair. Everybody deserves to fulfill this handsome stylist fantasy at least once.

But then roadblocks began to appear. I brought him to a dinner with the Billy-Bobs, and they took me aside, saying, "A little country, don't you think." They meant that while Jason was certainly lovely and sweet, he had no real intellectual pursuits (though very bright), and his subjects didn't always agree with his verbs. Some people would have made him into a project, but I'm not one who believes in trying to reform their partners, because I don't really think it works.

I discovered later that sweet Jason had a history of going after college professors from the area, always with the same results. He became just slightly bitter about their initial attraction to his exceptional looks, resulting, however, in failed affairs (Jason didn't hunt for one-night stands). Our dating awakened for a very brief spell a couple of years later, but Jason eventually became the domestic partner of another stylist with excellent business sense. They opened their own shop together and did very well. Bumper cars: just press the accelerator and aim for the next target.

The other stylist I dated, Rolland Hunter, possessed many of the same personality traits as Jason, and he exploded like a compact bundle of dynamite in bed. He had curly, strawberry-blond hair on his head, on his chest, and elsewhere, I discovered the first night he picked me up. His morning stubble (always shaved immediately) grew out red, and he sported a rhinestone stud in each ear, both omens of things to come.

Rolland had a singular education: he had trained as a piano virtuoso at a prestigious northern conservatory, and he not only liked the Rachmaninoff *Rhapsody* but could play it exceptionally well, along with a good many other major pieces. A nine-foot concert grand conspicuously graced his apartment. Unfortunately, the world has an oversupply of talented pianists, and reaching the concert stage takes luck as well as talent. The life of a supply musician didn't provide a very good living, but hair dressing did.

Rolland oddly lacked much free time. Both of us were unavailable during the week, of course, but my new boyfriend was also occupied many weekends. It took me about two months to discover why he should be so scarce when everybody else relaxed. Andrew delicately steered me to enlightenment as if through the intrigues of the Romanov court. "Are you seeing Rolland this weekend?" he asked innocuously.

"No, he seems to be busy. In fact, he's busy a lot of weekends, but not at the salon," I puzzled.

"Then, why don't we go to the disco on Sunday night, since you're not otherwise occupied. Let's make it early, so we can return at a reasonable hour."

"Sure," I answered unsuspectingly.

Now, I rarely went out on Sunday nights. Just then I sang with the church choir, and I tried to get home on Saturdays by 2 AM at least. After services on Sunday I needed to rest and prepare class for the following week. But this one time couldn't hurt, I reasoned. Andrew and I arrived at the disco about 7 PM, and that's when the drag show started. I wasn't particularly fond of drag; some of the performers had a good deal of talent, and they spent a fortune on costumes. But as abstractly entertaining as it could be (*La Cage aux Folles II*, sequel to the original French movie, had appeared just the year before), I would much rather have seen go-go boys dancing in shorts than men in dresses. Still, I watched with some interest when the star of the evening, billed as Dolly Darling, entered in gold-sequined platform heels, a gold lamé gown, long blood-red nails with lipstick to match, an elaborately coiffed blond bouffant wig, and a pair of ornately dangling rhinestone earrings. Dolly proceeded to lip-sync expertly to her namesake's "9 to 5," released the year before.

"Look familiar?" Andrew asked.

I peered across the darkened room, "Not really."

"You're just in denial—look again more closely."

I examined the face under the wig and tried to imagine it without makeup, "Good God, it's Rolland!"

"Look on the bright side," Andrew offered, "If you need a female armpiece for a reception at the University, you're in luck."

"You're entirely insane, aren't you?" I replied. Andrew just smirked. "When did you cook this up?"

"When I saw him without the wig for the first time at your place two weeks ago. It's quite a disguise, don't you think?" He milked this for his amusement.

"Given your political fantasies, Prince Ivanov, I'd say you're skating on pretty thin ice," I shot back petulantly.

"Temper, temper. And I'm not a prince, my father holds the title."

"Why don't you use that one to apply for a visa at the Soviet Embassy. Because your family has no chance of reclaiming its ancestral estate. Besides which, the Russian Imperial Family descended largely from minor German royalty, if you hadn't noticed."

"Don't be disrespectful! I was just doing what best friends do—they alert."

"Thanks a lot. I really appreciate it. And let me return the 'alert': I understand that the KGB still has a contract out on the members of the deposed Russian aristocracy. And if they don't assassinate you, I might."

Of course Andrew needed to let me know that my current lover was a drag queen of no small talent. Still, disillusionment stings. As beautifully masculine a body and (unpainted) face as Rolland possessed (accompanied by talent in bed, intelligence, and culture), I could never quite dismiss from my mind the picture of him dressed exquisitely as a woman ("A little bit of powder, a little bit of paint, makes little Rolland everything he ain't"). The two personas seemed completely incompatible, and I couldn't reconcile the talented drag queen with the attractive and very unaffected man I dated. Consider this a sin, if you will, but I lost all passion for him after that (though I did try, since nothing on the male side had changed). Denied a venue for conventional performance, Rolland found an outlet for his ambitions on a different stage. Eventually, when I asked, he showed me his two closets full of clothes and accessories. I didn't disapprove, but every time I went to have sex with him, I saw Dolly not Rolland. "Put the bumper car in reverse and see what you hit," ran Andrew's perennial advice.

The next fellow I ran into at a gay bar seemed very promising at first. His name was Michael, a blond who looked something like Andrew, and he came with a comely, dark-haired sidekick, Frank. Both worked as florists in the same shop; they had been friends since grade school in one of the local towns not too far from Pulpitville.

Michael spoke well, and he avidly followed old films (his passion) and pre-50s popular songs (he had no use for disco). He also made a good weekend companion (unlike Andrew, Michael did not play dead between the sheets). We often went out to dinner, shopping, and out to the movies. In most of these activities Frank accompanied us. This became a little odd, recalling a song by the 20's matinee idol Ivor Novello:

I seem to be the victim of a cruel jest,
It dogs my footsteps with the boy I love the best.

He's just the sweetest thing that I have ever known,
But still we never get the chance to be alone.

We see a film show—And his brother comes too!
Asked *not* to do so—Still his brother comes too!
He simply can't take a snub, I go and sulk at the club,
Then have a bath and a rub—
And his brother comes too!

There may be times when couples need a chaperone,
But brothers ought to learn to leave a chap alone.
They should have a heart and use their common sense,
For three's a crowd, and more, it's treble the expense.

Not entirely accurate—Frank paid his own way. Neither was he hard to be around. He had very good looks, ironically bearing a strong resemblance to the utterly gay Novello. But Frank's constant presence struck an out-of-tune note.

Nor did Frank play anything like a chaperone in the end: it turned out that he had no apparent objections to sloppy seconds without Michael around. Frank phoned one Saturday afternoon to chat when he knew his comrade was working. We talked for a bit, and then he asked, "So when are we going to get it on? Michael says you're good," thus adding a coda:

> And when they're visiting me,
> We finish afternoon tea,
> He loves to sit on my knee –
> And his brother does too!

Danger, Nick Walker, danger! "Well, I'm busy this

afternoon. Can I get back to you on that one." But I didn't, of course. I briefly entertained the notion that the pair always worked this way, but then rejected it. Michael seemed too conventional. I could have told him about my conversation with Frank, but why ruin his long-standing friendship with his former schoolmate? So I did the courageous thing: I ran. I made no more dates with Michael and Frank (in tow), and I swore off florists, perhaps unjustly. I had nothing against loose morals (don't say it: you already knew that, so spare me your disapproval). But I didn't want to sail between Scylla and Charybdis in quite that way.

The last great hope in the vein of more mature romance during my early 30s appeared in the form of appealing Chuck, a resident of Pulpitville, graduate of the University, and clerk at a local bank. He took my fancy the first time I saw him in church, a former fraternity brother in khakis (the other students on campus labeled them "fratty baggers" because of their relatively loose-fitting pants in a period of tight jeans). This garb was familiar to me from prep school, which many of the frat men had attended: they all possessed the standard blue blazer and rep-striped tie in school colors. In short, I felt an immediate affinity with Chuck. More cute and easygoing than handsome, he even played bridge quite well. He also made appearances at the bars in the towns around Pulpitville, and I thought he'd offer fun appropriate to my crowd.

Chuck was about my age, and he still paid occasional visits to his old frat house, where I imagined some of the brothers so inclined had a go with him. Our initial dates went normally enough, and since we had just begun to explore, I didn't think much about his day job as a bank clerk or the nights he spent with his other friends. Within a short time I developed a very deep crush on the man, who seemed closer to kinship material than anybody else I had met thus far.

Then one night when we left the bar, Chuck invited me back to his apartment, adding, "This is my friend Tony. I'm giving him a lift home." It fell short of full disclosure; my ex-frat crush should have explained, ". . . to my place." Now you've already seen that I had no fundamental objection to three-ways (or four-ways or random groups). True, the lacrosse scrimmage had tested my endurance. But I confess that I had celebrated one Fourth of July in Pulpitville by bringing home two young hitchhikers for a spirited session—tipsy straight boys up (to put it mildly) for a little experimentation. Amazingly, they called their girlfriends to fetch them in the morning. At all events, Chuck's friend Tony was also cute and enthralled by Chuck.

It turned out that Chuck had much more in mind than I bargained for. I had never seen Chuck's apartment, and I immediately became thankful for my ignorance when I walked in. Fast-food wrappers littered all the tables and kitchen counters, the shower grew some organisms that might have interested the biology department as samples of mutated species, and the bed clothes had gone unlaundered for a couple of weeks at least. A straight female friend of mine once characterized all gay men as fastidious; I laughed at this stereotypical myth and never let her forget it. Gay men exhibit the whole range of male domestic order or disorder. But Chuck's household chaos portended something more: he and Tony wanted not only to play but also to shoot up. They stripped, Chuck hauled out his bag of cocaine, mixed some of it with water, took out a tourniquet, wrapped it around Tony's bicep, and pushed a hit right into his friend's outstretched arm. Tony returned the favor for Chuck.

"Want to try?" my aging fratty bagger asked.

"Don't think so," I replied.

"Probably just as well—when we get high we lose it, and we want you to help us out."

Ah, I would provide stud service. I was all too happy to try that out on both of them, though Tony blanched when he saw what I proposed to inject in him. I had a fairly good time, though when I left I vowed not to spend another moment on those sheets. I worried for a while afterwards, but I contracted no noticeable maladies from this encounter.

Still attracted to Chuck, I thought I'd try one more date. We went to dinner, and afterwards I took him home with me. But when we reached my bedroom, he immediately pulled out his bag of happy dust (drugs before sex). No needles this time, just inhaling a couple of lines. Not only did his snow have absolutely no effect on me (perhaps the white powder had been cut), but I truly did not want to go down that path (just as I didn't want to buy pot or Quaaludes). Legal alcohol sufficed, and it broke down inhibitions. It seemed the perfect drug of choice.

Later I learned that Chuck did a brisk business supplying his old fraternity house and several others on campus with various prohibited substances. Though other students indulged, the Greek houses had a particular reputation for a lot of drug use and drug dealing. This led every year to one or two memorable tragedies: a young man (usually) would attend a party, take some pills with alcohol, and die. His heart would simply stop, or he would become disoriented on a highway and run into a tree or a creek. And then from one of the local churches a procession of blue-blazered young men accompanied by their girlfriends would trudge back across campus to their chapter, having learned a sobering lesson too young.

Chuck, unfortunately, had not heeded the warning, and regretfully I gave up his company, though we'd greet each other cordially when I encountered him at the bank or on the street. Our failed romance turned out to be a stroke of good fortune, for me at least. Soon, we had no idea then how soon, we would all learn sobering and cautionary new lessons about the fragility and transience of life to our intense sorrow.

9 THE DIN OF ONSET

He shuffled into church from a side door on a beautiful Sunday morning in the Fall of 1982, as I stood at the back with the rest of the white-surpliced, red-robed choir. Emaciated, in obvious discomfort, the elderly man advanced gingerly up a side aisle, clutching a cushion to his chest with his right hand, using the left to steady himself on the rail of each successive oaken pew. Occasionally he hesitated or stopped altogether, breathing heavily. Perhaps he feared that the next step might precipitate a fall at the bottom of which he would simply crumble into dust. The whole congregation watched anxiously until the gentleman reached his destination at the end of the third pew. There a younger man, most likely a son, waited. He took the cushion and placed it on the hard bench to render an hour's worth of sitting bearable for his gaunt companion. The aged parishioner, his abundant gray hair recalling faintly its former blondness, looked vaguely familiar. But I couldn't place him, though I knew most of the congregation by sight.

The rector, compassionately attending to this painful scene, finally signaled the crucifer to start our procession. The hymn rang out incongruously, "All things bright and beautiful, All creatures great and small, All things wise and wonderful, The Lord God made them all." We moved up the center aisle to the raised stalls at the front and progressed dutifully through Morning Prayer. During a lull in the service, I asked the chorister seated next to me, "Ellen, who is that man down there, sitting on the right aisle in the third row?" She looked over discretely but couldn't identify him either, adding in her reply, "At that age the poor soul may not be long for this world." And that proved true: he was not quite 29.

The unpleasant shock of recognition came only a week after I had puzzled over the identity of the mysterious old man in church. I attended a dinner party at the Billy-Bobs, and seeing the gentleman at the far end of the table, I took Billy aside to ask, "Who is that?"

Billy guided me into the kitchen, out of earshot of the other guests, "That's Greg. The man seated to his left is his boyfriend, Chase."

"It can't be! Greg's in his late 20s."

"That's Greg all right, and he's very ill."

"From what?"

"They don't know," Billy shrugged.

In stealth and unrecognized, AIDS had slipped insidiously into the confines of Pulpitville, expressed first in a man little younger than I, whom I knew very well indeed. Like many of the men in my generation, Gregory had just attained some professional standing, in his case as an associate in a local law firm. Bright and eager, unencumbered by wife or children, he worked long hours and, like the rest of us, garnered a salary sufficient to enjoy travel in his few days off. His new-found affluence paid for weekends in D.C. or New York, where a vibrant gay scene thrived. Not the least of its recreations entailed nights out at the many lively bars where one could meet prospective boyfriends or simply one-night stands. We were young and we wanted to embark on all the adventures of life, each according to his own taste.

Greg was particularly active in the big cities and in the area surrounding Pulpitville too. When I traveled to D.C. or New York, I often saw him in the haunts of gay men. My friends in both cities regarded him as ubiquitous in the weekend scene, with many one-night stands, visits to the baths, the P-Street Beach, the back rooms of bars. He had an enormous sexual appetite, far outstripping mine (which obviously was considerable). Though not ruggedly handsome, under his blond hair lay the face of an androgynous angel such as Saint-Gaudens might have sculpted.

> On the lake where droop'd the willow,
> Long time ago,
> Where the rock threw back the billow,
> Brighter than snow,
> Dwelt a lad beloved and cherished
> By high and low,
> But with autumn leaf he perished,
> Long time ago.
>
> Rock and tree and flowing millstream,
> Long time ago,
> Bird and bee and blossom taught him
> Love's spell to know.
> While to my fond words he listened,
> Murmuring low,
> Tenderly his blue eyes glistened,
> Long time ago.

Tender blue eyes and angelic features accompanied

real ability: Greg's oral talents were unsurpassed on the Eastern seaboard. His fame extended to the local frat houses, where he would call to see if anybody needed relief at the moment. He cruised the library, the campus, and the local shopping malls to obtain the delicacy he sought. Anybody he serviced came away elated and grateful, quite willing to repeat the experience at some future date. Everybody in gay Pulpitville under the age of 35 had a brief encounter or two with him, and I was no exception. One friend characterized him enviously, "Greg's like McDonald's: a billion served." Along with Leporello in *Don Giovanni*, many men, straight and gay alike, kept a tally. (You've noticed astutely that I'm presenting part of mine here. How like a typically defective male.)

Now, I provide this semi-statistical detail as a matter of history, not indictment. It only took one encounter to contract HIV. But at the onset of the "gay plague," before anybody knew about retroviruses, all sorts of theories circulated about the origins of the "syndrome." Too many poppers, too many tricks, too little sleep—these were all reasons why people's immune systems disintegrated. And if any of these had validity, then Greg made a likely candidate for malaise.

During the first year Greg's personal physician had no idea why he took ill, and neither did any specialists. He had liver cancer, one clinic advised. They ordered a biopsy, which came back negative. Then somebody in our crowd claimed that in the process of biopsy the doctors had nicked an artery in the liver. That's why Greg aged prematurely, wasting away like some mummy already desiccated for the linen wrappings that would enshroud him in the dark tomb.

Finally Greg switched practices and went to the same general practitioner I coincidentally used for my checkups. The good doctor asked one simple question, "Greg, are you gay?" He replied affirmatively. And the wise man, who did nothing more complicated than read CDC mortality bulletins and *The New York Times*, declared, "I think you have Acquired Immune Deficiency Syndrome." Indeed, as early as 1980 people in the medical community began to hear about a mysterious wasting disease spreading through the gay population in large cities, especially New York, Los Angeles, and San Francisco. Before any report appeared in the wider press, some straight friends, who worked at hospitals in New York, warned me not to go "catting around—there's something out there," they disclosed ominously.

The debate continued to rage, and it would take a few years until virologists in France and the U.S. isolated and identified the cause of the disease. Not until then could they develop a test for the infection or determine how it spread. But without any identifiable cause, the gay community, at the beginning most afflicted, fell into several camps holding diverse opinions that prompted various reactions. At parties some friends would tease, "Is that a dark patch on your skin?"—a reference to Kaposi's sarcoma that none of us had yet seen in Pulpitville (and in fact I never beheld except on TV). Most people thought drugs, not some organism, determined the onset: bad downers, bad speed, bad cocaine. This had nothing to do with denial but simply betokened confusion.

At a dinner party Andrew and I jointly threw (he providing the fancy cooking, I the wine and the venue), some of our crowd brought along visiting Washington friends who worked for the NIH. They assured us that the only logical explanation lay in a virus of some sort (since antibiotics could cure some of the horrible secondary scourges that accompanied cases but didn't arrest the relentless immune collapse of people such as Greg). If it was catching, then we'd all have it, some at the table scoffed. We were highly active, we kissed, we had sex, we sweated in gyms together, we ate together, washed each other's dishes, clothes, bodies. It couldn't be communicable. The young gay researchers from NIH persisted, "What else can it be?" So should we give up our roommates, our dinners together, our socializing and sex? I wouldn't countenance this option: it denied life itself. "Die young and leave a beautiful corpse," Andrew maintained. But Greg's rapid wasting gave lie to the second half of that cavalier bon mot. For this reason, a few people among our group simply withdrew completely from the scene and became celibate.

As the various theories rose and fell, the danger seemed remote, then all too near. Greg, the sole local victim identified so far, continued to suffer a series of physical losses as painful as crucifixion but slower in final outcome. Though I knew Greg but slightly, I made a point of acquainting myself with his boyfriend—Chase was in his mid 30s. And when I first asked at church about Greg, he burst into tears. After he regained his composure, he told me, "It's the hymns I can't get through them without choking up."

"Is there anything I can do?"

"Do you work?"

"Yes, but I'm available weekends."

"Help me take him shopping or out to lunch. Or better yet, you go, just the two of you, while I clean up at home. I'm so tired."

"Can I do some of your grocery shopping?"

"Great, I'll give you some cash and a list." Greg and Chase didn't lack for money: Chase still worked and Greg had disability insurance. Greg also received excellent if futile medical care, his firm continuing him on their policy as a gesture of compassion. Chase, however, was running on emotional empty. I and a whole cadre of friends formed an informal support team, from graduate-student ex-tricks to young professional ex-tricks, a far-flung and quite capable group collectively.

We serially accompanied Greg, or Greg and Chase together, out for shopping, out to medical appointments, out to lunch, out to movies (if Greg could sit that long), invited them over for dinner—whatever we could devise to relieve the tedium and lend a sympathetic ear. We couldn't think of anything else to do.

The doctors were at a similar loss and watched with dismay and alarm as each new malady—the names of which the rest of us had never heard, let alone knew existed—presented itself. What were pneumocystis pneumonia (PCP), toxoplasmosis, candadiasis, cryptosporodiosis, mycrobacterium avium complex (MAC), progressive multifocal leukoencephalopathy (PML)? Greg was dying from a cascade of obscure acronyms. He was admitted for each one to the hospital, where the concerned staff put him in isolation, burning his mattress after each stay. Friends' visits involved donning a mask, protective eye shields, and a protective gown, which were deposited outside the door, also for burning, as if the Black Death had called. It wasn't so much "the gay disease" as "the gay terror."

Out of the alphabet soup of afflictions came another tongue twister: cytomegalovirus, sporting another abbreviation, CMV. With no available treatment, Greg went completely blind, the cruelest indignity of all for somebody whose livelihood depended on reading and writing briefs and who also loved books. Because he couldn't select literature, we brought whatever we thought would entertain. I picked Dickens, Le Carré, Waugh, Forster, and finally Dinesen. He bore all visits patiently, never complaining of his discomfort (at the end he suffered from terrible bedsores), glad of the company and a human voice to fill the darkness. I recall the last thing I read to Greg, a short section from *Out of Africa* entitled, "I Will Not Let Thee Go Except Thou Bless Me." And as I left, I received that blessing, "Thanks for stopping by. Come back soon." But death came more quickly and mercifully.

Then we all found ourselves in church again, I in a choir that had volunteered to sing for Greg's funeral. We processed down the center aisle, this time his coffin following us, as a deacon with a resonant voice chanted, "Lord, now lettest thou they servant depart in peace." Later we sang that most beautiful anthem, with its gently cross-rhythmed duplets and triplets:

> Everything becomes so still,
> The even's sighing disappears,
> Just then one hears beyond each hill
> The tread of angles drawing near.
> And all around the hollows fill
> With twilight's deeply spreading dark;

> Cast off, my heart, thy every ill
> And fear's oppressive mark.
>
> Above, black heaven's vault doth fill
> With glitt'ring stars' majestic light,
> The golden chariot's orb doth still
> Retrace its own abiding flight,
> As with the stars, it always will
> Illume thy pathway through the dark;
> Cast off, my heart, thy every ill
> And fear's oppressive mark.

My friend Ellen again stood beside me, as she had on that first day when I had seen but failed to recognize Greg. She looked out over the congregation, composed now mainly of virile, affluent men in their 30s, all dressed in dark suits, and whispered to me enviously, "What a waste!" For she had been dating, as I had, without notable success. As if in confirmation of her dismay, the undergraduate crucifer and alter boy, one of Greg's friends, wept inconsolably.

The minister began his homily, "Gregory led a very unusual life. But then, we all lead unique and unusual lives. We must all suffer and die and question at the last, 'Is it nothing to you, all ye who pass by? Behold and see if there be any sorrow like unto my sorrow?'" *Yes,* I answered to myself, *it is something to me, a great deal. And no, I have never felt such helpless sorrow.*

At the end of the service, outside the church in a courtyard, I approached Greg's father waiting as his son's coffin was loaded into a hearse. He didn't know me at all, but I said to him, "Your son was so courageous." He broke into sobs.

Over the next fourteen years I watched over two dozen of my friends move slowly, painfully, ineluctably to their last ends. The only period in my life I read obituaries lasted from 1982 to 1996; I can't bear them any more. Every five or six months the name of somebody with whom I had partied or had dinner or danced appeared in those columns, the cause of death unspecified but well known. Some of those men I tried to help in small ways as best I could; most slipped away after returning to their childhood homes.

Their obituaries, like the hundreds and eventually thousands statewide I did not know personally, revealed themselves by reading between the lines:

> Kenneth S, 32, formerly of San Francisco [or Washington or Chicago or New York], beloved son of Lillian and James S, died after a long illness in his hometown of Werlin, Tennelina. He is survived by sisters Margaret and Eleanor, in addition to his parents. Visitation at the Farrington Funeral Home from 6-9 PM Friday evening. Funeral at the Calvary Baptist Church 10 AM Saturday morning. Interment in the Calvary Church Cemetery, reception to follow in the Calvary Fellowship Hall. In lieu of flowers . . . .

The constant procession of death notices became like John Donne's bell tolling incessantly for all of us.

These young men (the oldest among my acquaintances was 42) knew what lay before them, they submitted to remedies that temporized but did not cure. They endured multiple torments either from their maladies or their fruitless treatments. They suffered acutely. But

I never heard one of them express fear. They remain the bravest men in the face of physical pain and certain death I have ever known. And their courage left all of us who remained with survivors' guilt and a muted variety of post-traumatic stress syndrome that would persist for the rest of our lives.

As we disrobed in the choir room after Greg's funeral, Ellen turned to me and said, "We need to get really drunk." That worked for me. The phrase "In vino—or scotch—veritas" hit the mark squarely: all of us needed to reassess the way we lived. And for me Greg's passing proclaimed a turning point—that time in a gay man's life during his early 30s when he asks whether there might be something beyond the discos and bars, careless liaisons, marriage on Friday and divorce on Sunday afternoon. I had casually sought something more enduring but found nothing. Where could I search that I had not already explored?

10 *QUEM DILIGIT ANIMA MEA*

The arrival of the plague—capricious in its choice of victims, silent, mysterious and utterly fatal—coincided with something like a biological clock not only within me (yes, men have these too) but without as well. For I looked in the mirror now and beheld an adult professor, rather than the post-doctoral student who had arrived carelessly unattached five years before. And then, my life had grown a little more isolated when Andrew Ivanov departed for a Fulbright in Rome the summer after Greg died. I had also moved out of the colony at Barker Commons and into one half of a duplex in a remote part of Pulpitville. All the more reason to find a new friend and a possible mate. I thought myself not unlike the singer of ancient times:

> By night on my bed I sought him
>   whom my soul loveth;
> I sought him, but I found him not.
>
> 'I will rise now, and go about the city,
>   in the streets and in the squares
>   I will seek him whom my soul loveth.'
> I sought him, but I found him not.
>
> The watchmen that go about the city found me,
>   to whom I said,
> 'Saw ye him whom my soul loveth?'

Just when I gave up compelling a result to my search, however, success presented itself unbidden. Not at endless parties and dances but in the main library one night after the end of first semester, when I was heedlessly returning a volume and looking for another, I discovered him returning a book also.

Now the stacks of the library at Pulpitville University had a reputation for random encounters. The shelves of books, the odd layout, and stairwells circulating between floors hid myriad nooks and crannies, and one could also make eye contact over the rows of literature. Some men wandered the floors with cruising solely in mind; I had done so too on various occasions with sporadic results. But I trudged down the length of the quads on that cold night just to finish the term's business when most everybody had departed for Christmas break. In mid December, a Tuesday, I expected to complete my errand uneventfully and return home for the last few days before I drove back to Chicago. In those years while my parents both still lived, I would spend a couple of weeks visiting, not incidentally hitting the watering holes in the city with gay friends.

As I hunted for a book on the fifth floor, a young man rounded the end of the row, and when I looked up, his face registered astonishment, his eyes widened, and then his whole being softened, as if he had let down the barrier that we all erect for encountering strangers. Slender and not very tall, he possessed sweet features, not ruggedly masculine but not softly feminine either beneath his abundant curly auburn hair. I must have registered something like the surprise he radiated. And I believed something then I never had before: that one could fall in love at first sight. It's a cliché my undergraduates never credited. But I stand here to witness that it happens largely in chance encounters such as one finds in a Hofmannsthal libretto, "Where have I ever been that I was so blessed."

> It was but a little that I passed the watchmen,
>   But I found him whom my soul loveth.

"Hi," he blushed, breathless.

"Hello. I was just looking for this . . . " I must have colored too, and for once I was almost completely at a loss for words, " . . . uh, book." *Oh Lord,* I thought to myself, *Do you have any more sparkling openers?* And when he stood there, immobile, "My name's Nick."

"Chris," was all he could manage.

Lacking any clever stratagem to continue, I asked lamely, still finding it hard to breathe, "Want a cup of coffee?"

"Sure. It's late. Where?" He smiled shyly.

"Well," I gulped, "How about my place?"

"Let's go. My car's in the lot; I'll follow you."

Once we came through the door, we didn't waste any time but proceeded right to the bedroom, and as he stripped his shirt off, he revealed a trim but nicely shaped torso, very like (I'm so predictable) John Kerr's in *South Pacific*. His body was completely smooth, the hair, silky to the touch, confined to the places that counted most. His skin possessed a beautifully supple delicacy. He in turn relished the exquisitely fine dusting of dark hair on my chest that had grown in my adulthood slightly short of meeting the almost imperceptible trail bisecting my midriff. We explored each other for as long as we could stand, then slipped between the sheets in great expectation.

I'd like to say that we made bed-shattering love, but that would exaggerate. While we kissed a lot and went through the motions with a modicum of success, both of us were so excited—though not remotely virgin—that we produced no physical earthquake. We felt an emotional one, though, and we slept quite contentedly holding each other until about 7 AM.

At that point he awoke, hugged me, and said, "Look, I'm driving back to my parents' place today. So I gotta get going."

"How about some breakfast?"

"Okay."

I went to the kitchen and whipped up some buttermilk pancakes. Chris marveled as if I had performed some sort of magic trick, "You can cook!" If there exists no other reason to live in the thrall of men, if they didn't have the bodies and scents and frame of mind I adore, their gratitude at being fed might well suffice. Chris was hungry and ate a couple of stacks, washed down with some coffee.

We found out a little bit about each other while we were eating, "Are you a graduate student?" Chris asked.

"No, faculty. Professor in the History Department. You?"

"Graduate student in English. First term. (He was 21). Professor, huh? Really?"

"Yes, just turned 33," I confessed, anxious that it would sound almost prehistoric.

"Even better. I like older men . . . uh, I mean more mature men . . . uh . . . you don't look it," he diverted his gaze shyly to the floor, hoping he hadn't offended me.

"Doesn't matter to me if it doesn't to you."

"If they had any English professor like you, I would have been all over the guy the second I arrived for classes." He paused as if to collect himself. "Hey, I need to hit the road. Here's the number at my parents'. Last name is Caldwell. My family lives outside of Philadelphia. Call me over break." He wrote the number down, "Where're you going for Christmas?"

"Chicago. Here's the number at my parents' home. They go to bed early in the evening, so call before then. Oh, my last name is Walker. When do you return?"

"Right before the beginning of the term. We need to get together as soon as we're both in town again."

"Agreed. And I'll call you before then in Philadelphia."

"Deal. Talk to you soon." And he exited the front door, climbed into his rather large upscale station wagon with red-leather seats (his parents had given him an old family car), and disappeared.

Now trading phone numbers usually means nothing. "I call you" is actually the number one gay lie; number two doesn't count, because I like protein, and number three has no validity (who's going to send me checks in the mail, anyhow?). Giving out your parents' home number has a somewhat different significance, but I didn't think much about it. I had the rest of the week before I drove off on Saturday. On the road thoughts of Chris—his face, his hair, his manner of speaking, his body, his soft skin against mine as we dozed through the night—kept resurfacing and circulating in my mind. I had had crushes before, but this one lay on a different plane.

On Sunday afternoon I arrived at my parents' home, and on Monday I thought I had waited long enough (more than the statutory three days). I called the number Chris gave me and reached (sigh) his mother, "Is Chris there. It's a friend of his from school, Nick."

The elegant and formal voice on the end of the line replied, "Christopher is out for the evening. But I'll tell him you called. Does he have your number?"

"Yes, I'm in Chicago for break," I tried not to let disappointment show in my voice.

"I shall leave him the message." His mother had no way of knowing that her son was gay, I guessed, let alone that I had called to touch base with him because I was already smitten.

The fates moved in no kinder ways the next night, for I went out with friends, and when I returned, I found my mother waiting with a message. Now by that time my parents knew about my love of men. And though I lived so far away that they couldn't observe my social life directly, they could draw reasonable conclusions.

My mother couldn't conceal her curiosity, "A friend of yours from Philadelphia called, a certain Chris?"

> I held him and would not let him go,
> Until I had brought him into my mother's house,
> And into the chamber of her who conceived me.

An involuntary smile lit my face, "Thanks for the message." I tried to leave it at that, but I recognized in her clipped, German-accented speech the preparations for an interrogation, the responses to which she really didn't want to hear.

"How old is this boy, Nikolaus?"—she regarded every male under 40 as a boy, and she only used the full German version of my name in admonition.

"He's almost 22."

"Don't you think that a little young?"

"How much younger are you than Father?" I had her there, and just to make sure she registered my point fully, I reminded her, "Now, let's see, you were 21 when you first met him? He was, ah, 32?"

"It happened during the war."

"Which meant, Mutter . . . ?" I too could admonish by using German, if she wanted to play that card.

This gave her pause for thought but didn't entirely halt the proceedings, "Should I meet this young man?"

"Perhaps. We'll see," and the smile on my face just kept spreading. "Anything else?"

"He said he'd call you as soon as he returned to school," she surrendered.

I couldn't hide my elation, but I had to suppress my impatience, so I left it at, "Thanks for the message." Which buoyed me for the rest of the ten days I spent with my parents. Leaving early to return would do no good; I needed to endure the agonizing wait.

Nothing quite equals the exquisite suffering that accompanies the expectation of a phone ringing. Before the advent of email and the cell phone's instant gratification that we now enjoy (or suffer), the suspense could last for days. I arrived back in Pulpitville on a Wednesday, knowing that Chris would drive back into town on Thursday. I didn't sit on pins and needles but on nails and spikes awaiting his call that Thursday afternoon. And I busied myself with any trivial activity to keep my mind off the anticipation: cleaning the refrigerator (didn't work), sweeping the porch (useless), washing the woodwork (total desperation; no help)—anything but class prep, which left me too much time sitting alone with my thoughts (and using my right hand—okay, are you satisfied?). When would he arrive? Three, four, five o'clock. Would he even call?

> But the hours are lazy folk!
> Content to drag in indolence,
> Pull, yawning, at their tiresome yoke;—
> Move along, lethargic gents!

I refused to leave the house for fear of missing the fervently desired chiming (my body tingling all over). Did I make a leap to catch the phone when it rang at 4:30? That wouldn't exaggerate much.

"Hey, this is Chris. Is this Nick?"

"Speaking. Where are you?"

"Just pulled into my dorm room. Haven't even unpacked. How was break?"

"The usual. Glad to be back!"

"Me too!" And now I had to wait for him to ask the next question: tonight, right now, when, when, when?

"So I promised some friends at the dorm I'd go out tonight. Free tomorrow night for dinner, a movie?"

Was I free? In one sense entirely unengaged. In another enslaved to anything he had in mind. Any attempt at nonchalance would have failed miserably. "Nothing on my schedule," I replied altogether enthusiastically (only one more evening of right-handed anticipation).

"Great! I'll come by at 5:30 and we can go from there."

"See you then . . ." *and I hope for a long time afterwards.* How would I last until the next day? It was almost unbearable, but I bore it:

> Oh mistress mine, where are you roaming?
> Oh stay and hear! Your true love's coming
>   That can sing both high and low;
> Trip no further, pretty sweeting:
> Journeys end in lovers meeting
>   Every wise man's son doth know.

He drove up exactly on time in his battleship of a station wagon. And when he appeared in the doorway, a dimpled smile lighting his face like the glow from a holiday candle, I knew my memory had not misled me. He had dressed carefully in an elegant sweater and slacks, loafers, and a windbreaker to ward off the frosty night breeze. His face registered again that same amazement that marked our first chance encounter in the library stacks.

"Come in," I invited nervously. And when I had shut the front door, he moved close to kiss me, a little shyly but very arrestingly. There followed a date that obscured all others before it in distant shadow.

"Let's go. I think there's a show at 8:15, so we need to get to the restaurant."

"Let me grab my coat."

"You drive. That panzer out there burns enough gas to keep the town buses running for a month."

"Where're we going?"

"I know this quiet place, Fin & Feather. It's little tame—no meat and a lot of veggie items—but the kitchen's good," and he should have added, *the lighting low and romantic.*

When we arrived, I discovered Chris had made a reservation and asked for a table toward the back of the dining area, near some large plate-glass windows overlooking a courtyard. Miniature Christmas lights strung through the bushes and barren trees still illuminated the frosted lawn, as if to ensure that the celebration continued. He ordered a bottle of white, saying "Have anything you want. Dinner's on me."

"You don't need to do that."

"Yeah, I do. No more argument; after all, you've already cooked breakfast for me. If you like, you can take me to the movie." He wanted to impress me, and it worked. I always thought I'd be the one to buy the meal, but he meant to show his seriousness (point taken).

Over dinner I discovered that he had a background somewhat similar to mine: he grew up on the Main Line in Philadelphia, a suburban region rather like the Chicago North Shore. His father practiced internal medicine, his mother superintended a household staff (they inherited wealth far beyond my parents', apparently). Chris had attended a private academy for prep school just as I had. And as our conversation unfolded, we realized that we possessed identical social instincts and reflexes. True, he was younger (though not inexperienced, I had already learned), but he had a maturity beyond his years. He also liked to tease in way common in my family, which I much needed. I'm inclined as a college professor toward too much formality (you may have noticed), but Chris could puncture that balloon with just a couple of nicely placed words.

"Try using some slang. You talk like my mother."

"Ouch!"

"No need to thank me," he chuckled.

Chris also found the Southern Mystique risible, and he explained, "Look, I really *am* a Yankee, and this school reeks of empty pretension. Last time I checked, the war ended more than a century ago."

"Do you get that a lot in your department?"

"It's an English department. What do you think? Okay, Faulkner writes superbly, Styron can move me in deep ways, and there are others. But the continually retouched portrait of a faded belle pining for the bygone glories of 'daddy's plantation' simply bores me. Have you ever noticed that most 'great Southern writers' wind up either in LA or New York? People become transplants for a reason."

"Why did you come to Pulpitville for graduate school, then?"

"It's a good department; not saying it isn't. But the nativist bullshit runs so deep here, you need hip waders."

"I'm glad somebody else thinks so."

"Why do you work here?"

"Good history department, good job, and I work on international affairs: nineteenth-century German history—the growth of the nation state and that sort of thing."

"Oh, a specialist in militarism, huh?"

"Very funny. Actually, I like men in uniform. Maybe you should go to the show with some other professor. Or maybe you have some weird fantasy about being conquered."

"I'm not into subservience. Anyhow, who's buying dinner?"

"I'm not a cheap date."

"If I remember, last time I didn't even need to buy dinner to get you home, *Dr.* Walker. And *I* must be a cheap date—you just flipped some pancakes," he laughed, then reassured "But I guess I liked 'em."

"My friends call me Dr. Nick. And if you're on good behavior, you might rate more pancakes—or not. Depends, *Mr.* Chris."

"On what?"

"On the show."

"You must mean the movie," he smirked.

"Maybe."

"Well then, time to finish up. The 'show' starts soon."

Chris picked up the check, which he wouldn't even let me see, and I drove a couple of blocks to park nearer the theater (the night had turned quite cold by then).

The movie in question turned out to be *Starman* (the only thing showing in town). And while it may not make the list of greatest films ever, it seemed appropriately romantic. An alien falls to earth, and, stranded, takes the shape of a wife's recently deceased husband to make his way home. At first she's frightened, but then she falls in love him and mourns his departure. A chance encounter suddenly producing unexpected affection—themes that fell in well with our encounter.

When we reached the car and climbed in, I turned the heat up full, for Chris complained of the cold. As we drove back to my place, he laid his chilled hand flat, palm outstretched on the center console, and I placed my palm over his, "For saints have hands that pilgrims' hands do touch, and palm to palm is holy palmers' kiss."

When we reached home I invited for the sake of form, "Do you want to come in?"

"What do you think? But I need to get something from my car."

"What's that?"

"My overnight bag."

"You planned to stay the night?"

"If things went the way I hoped, not just the night."

"How long?"

"Ah . . ." he blushed, "The whole weekend?"

"I suppose I'll need a different menu for Sunday morning?"

"Yeah, and we can't spend hours on that, either."

"You have someplace to go?"

"*We* have someplace to go."

"Where?"

He hesitated and then confessed, "I have to tell you the truth. We attend the same church. I don't think you've noticed me, but I've been dying to meet you." He added hastily, "Um, the library at the end of break: that came just by chance, but I took it."

"I see." In previous years if I had been faced with this, I probably would have cut and run. But I just asked, "So there's a suit bag too?"

He offered very reticently, "Well, a blazer. I mean, I didn't want to get too serious."

"Naturally. All my dates stay the weekend and then come to church with me. They aren't serious at all."—

Because he was obviously embarrassed, I reassured, "It's great. We'll have fun. Just one thing: are you always this conniving?"

"When it comes to you I am."

"Let's get out of the cold." And when we moved inside, he embraced me for what seemed an eternity in the sweetest and most soulful way I can remember.

> What is love? 'tis not hereafter;
> Present mirth hath present laughter;
>   What's to come is still unsure:
> In delay there lies no plenty:
> Then come kiss me, Sweet-and-twenty,
>   Youth's a stuff will not endure.

I don't recall the sex from that night. It didn't really matter all that much, because all of a sudden I understood what it meant to fall in love and to be loved. It felt as warm as his soft, naked body wrapped around mine—protecting me against the cold wind etching night frost on the window panes—and his soft breathing beside me and the occasional reassuring pat on my thigh when he awoke briefly before drifting off to sleep again.

> 'I charge you, O ye sons of Jerusalem,
>   By the roes, and by the hinds of the field,
> that ye stir not up, nor awake my love,
>   till he please.'

11 *ANSCHLUß!*

Awakening love apparently entailed more obligations than just cooking buttermilk pancakes on Saturday mornings (with 100% maple syrup, if you please, nothing else would do, apparently). How much Chris had planned and how much just came by instinct I'll never know (and he didn't tell). For he believed that he could retrain his boyfriends, molding them and their habits to suit him. He began immediately by rearranging my Saturday-morning schedule in a way to which I had absolutely no objection. While I sat peacefully in a corner armchair in my robe, reading the paper, he'd walk up, kneel suddenly, and go down on me as if he had entered a hot-dog-eating contest on Coney Island.

"You have a dirty mind," I protested in vain—he just grinned up at me—"and I'm dirty all over. You go to the showers, young man." Where I soaped him all over, returned a little of the favor, then pushed him up against the tile and proceeded to stuff him from behind as I massaged him in front until we both had our fill. We then had to clean up all over again. "Is this going to become a regular habit, or just an occasional one?" I inquired in mock protest.

"Every Saturday morning, most weekend nights and afternoons. Complaints?" I made none.

"What do you have in mind for the rest of the day?"

"Shopping, of course, because you can't wear those briefs. Did your mother buy those for you? (I blushed.) I thought so. Boxers only. Born free and free access," ran his initial declaration of sovereignty. After a visit to the local department store's men's accessories, I treated to lunch.

"Maybe a nap."

"Sure. Then we can go dancing tonight." Chris loved the disco almost as much as Cal did, something I would need to endure. Afterwards, with a night's occasionally interrupted sleep, we made it to church (which left no time for a morning romp, though not out of piety). He liked to sit with me because I had a decent singing voice for the hymns. But the weekend's idyll ended then and there. "I need to study," he explained as he decamped for his dorm room, I to dazed preparation for classes. But not before he insisted, "Next weekend." I did not resist.

For the rest of January he spent weekends at my place, and then began to expand the routine. He'd call during the week after he had finished his studying and ask to spend the night. This usually worked for me, though one week I came down with a terrible cold and tried to beg off, "You shouldn't come over tonight; I'm under the weather."

"All the more reason to keep you company. We don't need to do anything, but I can take care of you."

"You're just going to catch my cold."

"Isn't that what boyfriends do? I can make you tea (boiling water was pretty much the only thing he could handle in the kitchen besides washing dishes), I can cover you with blankets, I can take your temperature. We're supposed to suffer together."

"I'm really tired."

"Then we'll sleep"—in the buff, he should have added, because he insisted on this too.

"You're crazy!"

Anschluß!

"And aren't you glad?" He never did catch the cold.

When I asked him how he accounted for his frequent absences from his dorm room (he had a roommate he didn't much like), he just said, "Maybe the creep assumes I have a girlfriend."

"That might work for a while. But eventually somebody's going to notice us in church every Sunday and figure it out." He shrugged.

His frequent presence in my apartment led to further steps toward territorial occupation. Like Cal, Chris had a compulsion for neatness. "How long has it been since you dusted the Venetian blinds?"

"Never thought to dust them." I kept house but not obsessively.

Other questions followed. "How long since you washed the bathroom floor?" he disparaged. "When did you move the refrigerator last to clean behind it?" with a deprecating shake of his head. "Do you ever wash the windows? Who told you to fold towels that way?"

"Do I have a boyfriend or a maid service?"

"Both! Objections? I could charge by the hour."

"How much do you think that's worth?"

That would have offended some men, but he just shot me a mischievous grin and replied, "You can't afford the escort service. I cost way too much, so I'll comp that. As for cleaning and ironing, I'll exchange those for some cooking."

After Andrew departed for Rome, I had begun to study cooking seriously. And out of loyalty to my mother's birthplace, I started by teaching myself northern Italian cuisine from Marcella Hazan's *The Classic Italian Cook Book*, experimenting on Chris as I went. When I made dinner for him consisting of *fettuccine* in a sweet gorgonzola sauce (basically the Italian version of mac-and-cheese, heavy cream added for good measure), followed by squab stuffed with sage and liver, he was ecstatic, "Just like at home!"

I didn't know quite how to take this, "Really?"

"Yeah, really!" He dug in, "This tastes so good!"

"I thought you came from a WASP family. Caldwell's a British name, after all."

"Pretty much; Scottish too. But that's not the point. My father's family originally came from England, as did my mother's before the Revolution. But we have a Tuscan cook and maid who also served as our nanny, married to our Italian butler (*Butler?* I thought)."

"Chris, you didn't grow up with a crush on your butler?" I teased. "Did you fall for me because I look Italian?"

"Would there be something wrong with either of those?" he retorted a little sheepishly, adding with a grin, "It doesn't hurt that you can cook some of my favorite food."

As I observed before, sex and eating: men follow an entirely predictable pattern. I continued with items such as pasta in a cream-and-sausage sauce, a classic Bolognese, chicken cacciatore with wild mushrooms, crespelle stuffed with spinach, cheese, and prosciutto, lasagna with ham and mushroom sauce, squid braised in a tomato-and-white-wine sauce with porcini mushroom stuffing. Chris loved all of it, and I was an ever-grateful chef. To make matters perfect, he cleared away like maniac, washing the dishes and scrubbing the pots and pans. We had a lot of fun for dinner in those first months, and I discovered which meals truly pleased.

Anschluß!

My gay friends began to notice us often at the disco and in church together. We had clearly become serious about one another. And so the remnants of the separate-truce graduate students threw a formal dinner party for Chris's twenty-second birthday, black tie, fine wines, some of their best cooking. We grew into a couple, which felt good to him and to me.

After spring break (the week seemed like it would last forever; he called every day), he came back for the weekend. And in addition to his wardrobe (he was a total clothes horse) for the brief stay, he brought a small oriental carpet and planted it, like the emblem of an occupying country, in the middle of my bathroom floor. "There, that's better!" So now he was decorating my apartment.

I confronted him, "And this is?"

"A really nice Bokhara," he dodged.

"Which should live in your dorm room."

"Which should live on your bathroom floor, because it'll make things look homier when I move in at the end of the term."

"Who were you going to ask about that?"

"I already asked my parents if it'd be all right to live in an apartment with a roommate. Do you want me to call your mother?"

"Don't worry—the first time you answer the phone, she'll know exactly what's going on. She knows I'm gay. Does your mother know you're gay and will *she* know what's going on?"

"She thinks you're just a college buddy."

"I see. But were you going to ask *me*?"

"You don't have any choice. Either I move in or you pay the accrued charges for the escort service, which, as I've explained, you can't afford. And by the way, if you haven't figured it out yet, genius, I'm in love with you. You're my boyfriend, and I intend to make sure it stays that way."

He didn't settle just for retraining, he wanted *Anschluß*—annexation by ostensibly friendly forces. Unfortunately, he had me about the "in love" thing, because by that time I lived even more in thrall to him than I was when I first saw him.

> What magic hath victorious love
> For all I touch or see.
> Since that dear kiss, I hourly prove
> All, all is love to me.

I surrendered to everything: to his moving in, to his rearrangement of my closets, my dresser, my kitchen cabinets and utensils, my refrigerator, my furniture, and my life. I knew he really meant business when he reset the thermostat ("You keep it too cold, and I can afford to pay the utilities").

When the dorms closed in early May, he transported all of his clothes, his record collection, his books, and everything else he owned to my apartment. And he took sole possession for the first summer term, because I had a grant from the German government to spend six weeks abroad, pouring through the Munich State Library for documents relating to the Wittelsbach succession to the Bavarian throne. (Sounds dull, no? But the family history had entertainment value, especially eccentric Ludwig II, who was quite gay and also built elaborate palaces that came right out of deranged Teutonic fables).

Chris replied, when I explained this project to him, "No handsome Bavarians, royal or otherwise, for you buster. You're gonna write me every day, and we can talk on the phone once a week." That suited me fine, but I had this nagging vision of the house completely redecorated when I returned, with all of my furniture gone.

"How will you eat?" I asked.

"Order out until you get home."

It was a hard separation to endure just when we started domestic life in earnest. But it made him doubly happy when I returned in mid July. He had made a few more changes ("Where did you get those nineteenth-century celadon vases and that coromandel screen?" I inquired of my surreptitiously tasteful but entirely unresponsive interior decorator.) A new item or two would appear unexpectedly at intervals, slowly replacing the shabby furnishings I had accumulated since my graduate-school days. My mother noticed that I now had a live-in boyfriend, my landlord noticed, my colleagues noticed, and his graduate-student classmates noticed that we had become a gay couple when they began to see us out at movies. Even a couple of good-ol'-boy undergraduates next door accepted us as a pair and invited us to their kegger barbecues. The most entertaining of our neighbors, a retired couple who had downsized to a very modest house, invited us as partners to dinner (I think they may have fed Chris in my absence too).

All of this delighted me, and I decided we needed a honeymoon or two. Chris's family, for all their money, hadn't placed much value on travel, and I thought we could enjoy some relatively nearby sightseeing. Before classes began we took a trip to D.C., where in a long weekend we managed (I don't know how) to take in both houses of Congress before their August recess, the Washington Monument, the National Gallery of Art, the Freer Museum, the Smithsonian Museum of American History, the White House, Arlington National Cemetery, the National Archives, and virtually all the bars I knew around Dupont Circle. We were young and full of energy, and we danced into the night at Badlands, attending services at St. Paul's on K Street (where gay couples seemed to predominate at high mass during those years) before returning home completely exhausted but very happy.

"What do you want to do for fall break?" I inquired a couple of days later.

Chris didn't hesitate a moment, "New York: sightseeing, musicals—please musicals!"

"Have I ever told you that you have a lot of OGTs?"

"OGTs?"

"Obviously gay traits. These include items like interior decorating ('Guilty as charged.'), a disco fixation ('You could learn how to dance.'), and an overwhelming obsession with Broadway musicals," I teased. "Oh, did I mention sleeping with men."

"And limited to sleep after that speech," which summoned his arrestingly dimpled grin. "Okay, what's the plan?"

"You've probably hit all the tourist sites, no?"

"Actually, not. My parents didn't like New York. On the whole, they'd rather be in Philadelphia."

"Very funny. So we explore, see some musicals, and eat at my favorite places, hitting the bars at night."

"Don't worry about the budget. I can pay my half."

"You're a starving graduate student."

"Yeah, but my folks send me money, and I live with this older professor. (I shot him a dirty look.) I mean more mature—quit staring at me—uh . . . stunningly handsome grown man. Better?"

"Just watch it, my young friend."

I planned a comprehensive tour of the Manhattan I had begun to explore with Army-boy Wes when I was an undergraduate. We would stay at the New York Hilton in midtown, take in three shows, go dancing at some gay bars I had heard about (but never visited). We bought airplane tickets, booked the hotel, and Chris let me choose the theater menu.

We enjoyed ourselves immensely. He had never visited the top of the Empire State Building, the Statue of Liberty, the UN, the Metropolitan Museum of Art, Grand Central Station (still impressive if a bit shabby in those days), or Lincoln Center. For theater I chose *A Chorus Line*, *La Cage aux Folles*, and then surprised Chris with tickets to *Torch Song Trilogy*.

He protested, "Hey, I thought I said musicals only."

"Trust me, you'll like the play, and I'll treat you to dinner at Sardi's before the show."

It made for a special last night. Chris took one taste of the meat-filled crespelle at Sardi's and asked, "Can you make these at home."

"Sure. They're a variation on the crespelle stuffed with spinach that I already cook for you."

We both found *Torch Song Trilogy* deeply moving and P. J. Benjamin compelling in the lead. We went out to celebrate afterwards at Uncle Charlie's. But we couldn't stay out too late, because we had a flight to catch the next morning. I had impressed Chris, and he wanted to demonstrate his gratitude in a very tangible way when we returned to our hotel room, clearly in a romantic and oversexed mood (at 22 he was always oversexed). We stripped, fluffed a bit, and became very aroused.

"So, I know you like to play top dog, yeah?" he offered.

"Yes, and I'm about to try to make you pregnant again."

"How about the other way around?"

I considered for a moment, because I generally didn't like to be the catcher and had done it rarely. But I thought it ungenerous not to afford him the pleasure I enjoyed so much, "Okay. But I have to tell you, you need to go very, very slowly with me. I bruise easily, and it hurts."

"I won't hurt you, and I promise to go slowly; you're going to like this a lot. Go get a towel and lie on your back on the floor."

Hmmm, what was he up to? But I lay down obligingly. He *did* move very gently and slowly. And not only that, he fit me perfectly. It felt good.

But he wasn't finished with me at all, looking down impishly, "Bet you didn't know that I'm completely double jointed—everywhere."

"Double jointed?"

With him all the way in me, he bent down over my very stiff shaft and ingested me to the hilt while he gently slid in and out of me. (For those of you who suddenly started paying attention again: Warning—do not attempt this at home without the proper equipment!) If they have sex in heaven (which they should),

Anschluß!

it will feel like this. He kept mouthing me until I exploded, but he wasn't quite done.

"Just keep it up. I can last until you finish," I moaned. And when he finally climaxed I unloaded in his mouth again. This result pleased him (and me) immensely.

"How did you learn to do that!" I asked, breathless.

"Ah, well, I kinda thought it up."

"Can you do yourself?"

"No. If you haven't noticed, I'm not . . ." he blushed a little, "as big as you. Not that I'm complaining," he hastened to add. "In fact it's perfect. I can get into you and bend down to suck you for a long time."

"Can we schedule regular appointments?"

"It might be arranged."

"I suppose I need to be on good behavior?"

"Yep."

I became his abject sex slave, and we flip-flopped from then on. He'd arrive home at the end of classes, and after we had a couple of drinks but before we ate, he'd take me on the floor of the living room, in the guest bedroom, in our bedroom—anyplace that had a carpet. My usual assaults on him in bed also continued regularly. We lived contentedly, and I learned that lust felt so much better accompanied by love.

We spent Thanksgiving together, but parted for Christmas break. Not before our own celebration. He started giving me Waterford crystal (perhaps the last stage of the makeover), I gave him record albums (he particularly wanted Streisand's *The Broadway Album*) and some of the fancy polo shirts he adored. And when we returned, we contentedly spent another semester together, traveling for spring break to his parents' condo in Boca. As we relaxed on the beach, I thought everything had happened exactly as it should, with him sleeping in my arms:

> Oh eyes, oh blessed stars,
> The authors of my harms,
> That in slumb'ring wage wars
> To kill me with thy charms.
>
> When closéd you annoy me,
> When open you destroy me.

Yes, during summer break I'd go off to Germany again for six weeks while he taught classes in summer school (for he was now a senior TA). But we had survived this separation once; surely it would present no problem the second time. He couldn't redecorate the apartment again. And I felt secure. For as improbable as it had appeared during my first few years in Pulpitville, I had found somebody I might live with for the rest of my life.

12 THE MOST UNKINDEST CUT

When I returned in the middle of July after my Munich expedition, I imagined everything would resume as usual. Chris had a wonderful homecoming prepared. In private we behaved like sex fiends; in public we went out to dinner, to the movies, to the disco, and to some dinner parties of our friends, including the Billy-Bobs (whom Chris, like Cal, found interminably boring and generally useless). But significant trials lay in the offing. I would come up for tenure in fall term; Chris would need to pass the spring qualifying exams that determined whether he would continue for his Ph.D. Fortifying each other, we would endure.

We didn't realize at first that these crucial hurdles would create a divisive psychological torture. As an openly gay young couple in that homophobic desert, we would gain no comfort, quarter, or pardon from the Pulpitville establishment.

The process for granting tenure at a university descended from traditions as medieval as the institution itself. One compiled a dossier, including not only a curriculum vitae (every breath taken since college) but also copies of all publications, references from scholars outside the institution, student teaching evaluations, and instructional observations by faculty colleagues. If permitted, the powers that be would have required items such as blood tests, urine samples, fingerprints, home inspections—in short, anything and everything to make a "candidate" (read: victim) believe that he or she had given up his or her constitutional protection from unreasonable search and seizure.

After assembling this mountain of information (most of it superfluous), a candidate submitted it to four (count them, 4) levels of committee review: in the department (subject to a ratifying vote of all tenured faculty in that "unit"), in the office of the appropriate dean, in the office of the provost, and in the office of the president. All of these submitted provisional recommendations (yea or nay) that didn't become final until endorsed by a board of trustees and/or governors (depending on the institution).

The whole tenure process lasted about a year and resembled a trial by combat from the Dark Ages or (my favorite comparison) the trial of witches and warlocks by water ordeal. One way to discover a practitioner of unholy conjury involved throwing them bound and gagged into a deep pond. If they floated, they were guilty and sentenced to burn at the stake; if they sank and drowned, they were innocent. I came to think of the latter outcome as more humane by far than what I actually experienced.

Of course, a university would try to mitigate the appearance of *complete* barbarism created by this ordeal: in the spirit of sham democracy and fairness the victim had a choice of executioners. One could select certain members of the departmental tenure committee, the chair of the department chose the rest. One could nominate outside referees; the committee then chose from their list and from the victim's. All this the administration conducted in utmost secrecy until the tenured members of the department had voted, whereupon the candidate received a letter revealing a recommendation for or against tenure. But the upper-level committees could reverse this recommendation without giving any justification at all. Levels of appeal followed, most of them fruitless and token. University politics surrounding tenure reduced most junior faculty to some variety of psychotic paranoia.

In qualifying exams, Chris's department would test "candidates" (victims again) on everything one should know about English literature from Chaucer to Capote, dependent solely on the whim of the examining committee. The department appointed the committee (a victim hoped he or she had done well in a course with one of the five committee members), which then designed a series of essay questions answered over three grueling days (with breaks for lunch and evenings for frantic study) right before spring vacation.

Chris compared this procedure not to the water ordeal but to simple burning at the stake: "If I can blow the flames out quickly enough, perhaps I'll leave charred but alive." The trial elicited its own peculiar neurosis, but at least the misery had company. Graduate students would form study groups to divide the various periods tested into segments, with each member of the group producing study guides in his or her area for the others to use.

It was unfortunate that we both underwent these torments during the same year, and we reacted differently for different reasons. Once I had completed my dossier and submitted the extensive paperwork, I had nothing to do but wait. I became indolent, quarrelsome, and suspicious, a mood not improved by the fact that Robert Hastings (Little Boy Blue, the closeted sadist who used his network of former students to enlist hustlers in New York) wangled an appointment to my committee. Chris became preoccupied and increasingly secretive, a development intensified by the appointment of Aloysius Throckmorton (Frogman, the closeted English-Department predator) to his examining committee. You'd think our joint misery would have drawn us closer together, but it had the opposite effect.

Domestic friction marked most of fall term, small items at first that cumulated, in retrospect. First came social outings. Though I would go to the gay bar, I behaved elusively in other settings.

"Nick, wanna go see *St. Elmo's Fire* Friday night?"

"Okay, fine. Great. What time?"

"Let's catch the 9 o'clock." As with all popular movies, a lot of students were in the lobby when we arrived, including some of Chris's graduate-student friends. He'd try to introduce me, but I'd duck away, "Oh, I need to make a pit stop," leaving him to explain. After the show, he'd protest, "Those were members of my study group, and you should meet them."

"So you can show off your trophy-professor boyfriend?"

"Yeah, sure. You're a prize, all right, only not exactly the World Cup at the moment."

I looked down and confessed, "Chris, I'm up for tenure. They're going to spread our living together around, and it's going to get back to your parents, who in turn will call the department to demand I be fired for seducing and corrupting their son."

"Too late to sneak back into the closet, don't you think? It's not as if people don't see us in church every Sunday, at the movies, in restaurants, even at the occasional college reception. I always thought you were proud of me, but maybe not." His injured tone was all too apparent and completely justified. Nor had he finished, "As for my parents, you let me deal with them. And while we're on that subject, do you really think they'd like it better that you take me out to the bars?"

"That's different," I offered defensively, "Everybody there is gay."

"And that makes it all right? You suck, man."

"Oh, you've developed some sudden objection to that?"—an unnecessary barb.

"Maybe we could give that a pass tonight," came the huffy rejoinder.

We tried to live by the principle of never going to bed angry. I was ashamed of my behavior, apologized profusely when we returned home, and did everything I could to make him feel loved in all the ways he wanted. But these episodes began to strain our relationship. It showed when our gay friends came to dinner. He played his usual efficient scullery assistant, but I'd complain in front of company when he'd clean up a pot or pan rather than staying at the table. This drew a frown where he used to tease me out of my criticism. I started leaving dishes in the sink for him to deal with when he came back home because he hated it.

"Nick, you can't put your plates in the dishwasher?"

"I thought that was your department?" Another frown.

For his part, he'd indulge small subversive gestures, like changing the thermostat after I had left and then turning it back when he heard my car come into the driveway.

"Chris, did you turn the heat up?" I'd ask, as I walked on a chilly fall day into a place that was 78 degrees.

"No, take a look. It's set at 72," he lied.

"Then why is it so warm in here?"

He shrugged and went back to studying a book for his exams. From petty beginnings mighty quarrels grow.

His study group seemed to run later and later as the term moved on. Chris would try to sneak in quietly so as not to wake me, but I slept lightly and would let him know, "Long session tonight, huh?"

"Yeah, we have a lot to cover." I started pretending to be asleep when he stole back in, wondering how many times a week his study group could meet so late.

The term moved forward, full of miscommunication, some reticence, a little deceit mixed with insincerity and a dash of disaffection. Chris practiced avoidance as his main technique: he contrived not to be around much. My approach involved a steady stream of minor disparagement and complaint. We both understood that something had broken down, but we didn't discuss it, regarding it as "tact."

Into the midst of this dreary atmosphere came good news, or so it first appeared: the departmental committee had recommended me for tenure, but not unanimously. The letter from the chair didn't transmit the vote (which a sympathetic colleague on the committee leaked), just the outcome. Elated, I brought the glad tidings home to Chris in early November. He was sincerely happy, and he took me out for dinner. We had a favorite Chinese restaurant not too far away where we went to celebrate good fortune that arrived on the spur of the moment. He seemed very proud and truly pleased. We spent a happy Thanksgiving break together, and we prepared for our private Christmas party before we would both return to our respective families for the longer holidays.

Right after final exams finished for the term the bombshell landed. On a Friday afternoon I sat quietly reading on the sofa in the great room of the apartment when the doorbell rang. I opened it to find a delivery from the local florist, a vase full of two-dozen yellow roses, my favorites. I thought Chris had sent a special gift, that perhaps things were returning to normal. Touched, I unsealed the envelope, which had no name on the outside, to read the card: "Sweet Chris, Thanks for the great night! Looking forward to seeing you when you return from break!" It was signed "Evan." Evan? I didn't react immediately. I just set the abundant bouquet right in the center of the coffee table and placed myself behind it, idly leafing through a magazine on the sofa, waiting for Chris to return.

He walked in the door and remarked, "Beautiful!"

"Read the card—go ahead."

He pulled the envelope from the holder in the arrangement, opened it, read, let slip an embarrassed little giggle, and then flushed scarlet, "Nick, I, uh . . . , it's . . . "

"Who's Evan?"

"Oh, nobody who'd interest you."

"Please, I'm intensely interested," I raised my eyebrows with curiosity.

"Look, he's somebody I met by chance."

"In study group?"

"In the library, looking for a book one night," he squirmed trying to think what to say next.

"Sounds familiar. Been doing some outside research?" I asked in a quiet tone.

"A little. Nick, you've been so critical and difficult, and we haven't been . . . well the sex hasn't been that great, and I made a terrible mistake. I'm so sorry. Don't be mad at me. I'll stop. I don't love this guy, I love you!"

"Okay, I'll go with that one. But I'd be lying if I said this doesn't hurt a lot." I remained calm, which seemed to make him even more nervous.

"Let me take you out tonight to someplace really nice. Let's come back and open Christmas presents. I'll try to make it up to you."

One momentary lapse, I thought to myself. I sighed, "I'll take you at your word, but no more of this. For one thing, it's dangerous—for you *and* for me."

"I know! Thanks, Nick, thanks. You don't hate me?"

"I don't hate you; I'm just disappointed and upset. I know I've been really difficult; I'll try to be kinder."

We went out to dinner at a fancy French place in town (for which Chris footed an enormous bill), caught the movie *Out of Africa* (romantic in its way, but also cautionary in Karen Blixen's battle with syphilis), and returned to open presents. I had bought him clothes: a couple of the very expensive sweaters he needed to stay warm in the house, some slacks, a new camel-hair blazer. But he had outdone me with a very expensive Japanese screen for the wall of the apartment and a set of eight Waterford claret glasses he had ordered in advance for the collection he had started building for me. He apparently felt guilty even before the incriminating flowers arrived. We made up in bed.

The Most Unkindest Cut

When Chris and I returned from Christmas break, things seemed to go well at first. But a letter from the dean's office shattered our tranquility. It read, "Dear Professor Walker: I'm sorry to report on the decision of the College Personnel Committee. I cannot forward your file with a recommendation for permanent tenure." It went on to list the various appeals I might make, and it bore Giles Barnard's signature as dean. (You don't remember him? You might recall his alias: The Stripper—failed and kinked-out professors apparently become deans). The closet conspiracy (this clearly bore the stamp of Little Boy Blue's influence) had struck below the belt, so to speak.

Chris expressed dismayed, but I could also hear him begin to dodge, "Does this mean you'll need to leave at the end of this term?"

"No. However this turns out, I would at least have another year. You'd be done with classes by then."

"If I pass quals, but even then there's a dissertation. You might not last that long."

"I'm going to appeal. My credentials are better than anybody who's received tenure in the past three years. It's politics."

"Politics?"

I told him about Little Boy Blue and the Stripper (whom he already knew by his extensive reputation on campus), "They'll need to justify this decision, and I don't think they can. There's 'personal malice' involved."

"And you're going to use our living together to make that point? With my exams coming up in six weeks and the Frogman on the committee. Gee, thanks," Chris complained

"Now who's retreating back into the closet? Glad you're so courageous and supportive."

Chris began to protest, but then thought better of it, "You know I want you to have tenure. I just didn't think this would get so nasty."

"Well, it's going to become nastier." I could hear his apprehension, and our relationship already stood on shaky grounds. I grew a little more difficult to live with, in part because of Chris's continued "study sessions," which now lasted as a rule until 2 AM. My former acquaintances were dying with frightening regularity, two or three a year, and my live-in boyfriend apparently slept around frequently.

First things first, I thought. My father recommended I contact one of his former law-school classmates and a fellow vet—a good-ol'-boy Washington lawyer specializing in educational employment, one Carlisle Sithwell. I called him and he moved right to the point, "So let me get this straight. You have two fellas sneakin' around on their wives with guys on campus and off, and they know that you know, and also that your housemate and you . . . ya'll are . . . let's just say, pink?"

"Openly gay. I live with my boyfriend and socialize with him in public."

The lawyer answered shrewdly, "That's your best defense. I happen to have an undergraduate degree from Pulpitville, and as fondly as I recall my years there, I know how those folks work. There's no non-discrimination regulation about sexual orientation at the University, is there?"—a rhetorical question—"Well, let me tell ya, I don't think you even need me to call those fellas. Here's what ya do. Send me a check for $500 tomorrow, send a letter—registered, return receipt requested—appealin' the decision to your sorry-ass dean. What's his name, by the way?"

"Giles Barnard."

"Oh, that one," he reacted knowledgeably. "Schedule an appointment with ol' Giles and take along a sympathetic faculty colleague for that interview. Mention that you've retained me as counsel, and that you want a full investigation of the tenure decision. Tell him you may need to go to court, in which case you're goin' to call witnesses about personal malice. Just try that, and contact me if things don't go well. 'Cause I'm here to tell ya, son, there're many ways to skin a cat, lessin' the cat don't want its guts revealed, pulled out, and twisted into violin strings. In which case that cat's gonna run for cover. I moved away from Pulpitville 'cause I reckon they bury too many things there in dark places. They got a lot of stones that they don't want overturned." (You're thinking, this was blackmail? Not exactly—merely the prospect of revealing some inconvenient truths.)

"Don't you think there's a danger in using the same thing they're using against me."

"You're openly gay, right? You aren't cheatin' on anybody? No, it's fightin' fire with fire, or, if you like, usin' the same sauce on the goose you'd use on the gander. Now you go pour yourself a bourbon and branch water or maybe a scotch and soda, you bein' your Daddy's son. I'll hear how this went from him, I reckon."

"Will you relate our conversation to my father?" I asked anxiously.

A Chosen Landscape

"Well, our parlay is confidential by law. Your Daddy knows you're gay? (I remained silent on that point.) I thought so. But that doesn't make no never mind to me. Go on now, son."

"Thank you, sir"

"You can call me Lisle like your Daddy does."

"Yes sir, I mean Lisle."

"Rest easy, Nick. You're in good hands."

For a little more support I turned to Bob of the Billy-Bobs. I described the situation, and unsurprisingly he cleaved to the lickspittle party line, "You should just accept the decision." He followed two rules of University politics: "don't make no waves; don't back no losers." He proved as feckless an ally as he was a host. I would gain no support from the old timers at the University. But I did take a younger tenured member of my faculty committee as witness to a scheduled meeting with The Stripper, ah, Dean.

My interview, ten days later, proved instructive. I followed the script my lawyer had written for me, "Sir, I've come with a member of the tenure committee that recommended me, and I've also retained counsel on this matter."

The Dean leaned back in his chair, "That's hardly necessary at this point."

"Well, I want to make sure I'm treated fairly. Now on the advice of counsel I'm bound to tell you that should you not reverse your recommendation to deny tenure we'll file a brief in court alleging personal malice."

"Against whom?" he adopted a hostile tone.

"To begin with, against Professor Hastings, who's been sending me these lovely notes. (I displayed a pile of the scribblings he had placed in my box over the years)."

"But the History Department recommended you for tenure," the Dean asserted uncomfortably.

"The vote wasn't unanimous: one dissent."

"What would prejudice Prof. Hastings against you?"

"I'm openly gay, living with a partner."

The Dean shifted uneasily in his chair, "Go on."

"My attorney, Carlisle Sithwell, has advised me that this fact might arise during any civil proceedings. And I'd be forced to place these notes in evidence and perhaps to document a history of tension between me and Hastings through the testimony of some of his former graduate students now living in New York."

Barnard sat straight up in his chair as if a fire had been lit under his sagging behind, "Carlisle Sithwell? He was an undergraduate in one of my classes here. There'd be no need to call . . . "

"Oh, but I've been advised by Mr. Sithwell that we'd be forced to call witnesses to all the facts."

"But *my* committee made the decision."

"Then there'd be further witnesses to, uh, bare all the evidence on any connection between you and Professor Hastings." I gauged his discomfort by his color: at the word "bare" he blanched, but given his leathery brown hide, you couldn't say he turned white, just paled to the color of faggot beige.

"No need for that, I'm sure," he had to clear his throat before he could get this last phrase out. "Let me return to the committee for a reconsideration of your file. We'll be in touch."

"Soon?"

"Very soon!"

"Thank you, sir." I stood up and turned to conceal a smile. Ten days later the dean's personnel committee reversed their decision and recommended me for tenure. The other committees followed suit pro forma, and I gave the good news to my parents, then to Chris.

Though pleased, Chris was anxious about his own ordeal in a week. His on-going late-night "study sessions" produced a stream of letters sent to the house, no return address, perhaps from the same admirer who had sent the roses before Christmas. I passed over these in silence, hoping that when he had cleared his exams, he would calm down. He struggled through the three days, and then, unlike the year before, spent spring break with his parents in Philadelphia.

Disaster hit Chris when he returned for the remainder of the semester. He called me at lunchtime, asking to see me right away (something unusual). And when I met him in one of the more secluded sections of the library, he burst into tears, which I had never seen from him before, "They've charged me with cheating on my qualifying examination."

"Steady, man. Who's charged you?"

"Prof. Throckmorton and my former roommate."

"Did they give a reason?"

"They claim I looked on somebody else's paper."

"But it's an essay exam. It's not possible to cheat."

"Well, they're claiming it just the same."

"What possible reason could they have?"

"I refused to have an office 'interview' with Throckmorton to become his TA—you know, *that* kind of interview. And my former roommate then took the job. They all know about you," he offered, disconsolate.

I thought for a moment, then asked, "Do you think your former roommate had something against you? Or did he have a crush on you?"

"My dorm mate was such an unattractive slob, I never thought about him as gay."

"Given Frogman's tendencies, I wouldn't put it past him to ask for more than academic work from a TA. In any event, let me see what I can do. The honors people can dismiss charges, which they might do if I can persuade Throckmorton and his TA to withdraw their accusation."

"You think you can arrange a dismissal?"

"Perhaps. Do your parents know about this?"

"Yes, but I didn't give them details."

"Okay, just tell them you'll dispute the charges."

I made an appointment with Throckmorton, who received me in his office, reclining in his chair like an old bullfrog sunning himself on a lily pad. "Now what's this about, Professor Walker? You don't have any evidence to give in this matter, do you?"

I borrowed from my Washington attorney's playbook, "Possibly. You know that Christopher Caldwell lives with me."

"Yes, I see you in church with him."

"He asked me for advice, and I told him that a case before the honors board might involve testimony from other students I know, graduate students and undergraduates whom you've advised in the past. Perhaps also from your present TA? Chris feels their stories might have some bearing on his case."

Throckmorton's jowls quivered and he turned beet red, "That'd be entirely irrelevant. I don't see the connection! And I've heard about your tenure review."

"Resulting in a positive recommendation from the dean's committee, now before the Board of Governors for their seal of approval. Do you regard my and Chris's cases as related? That would be truly inappropriate—and admissible as evidence of bias."

"Listen, you guinea pissant, you're in waters far too deep for you to swim in!"

I formed a quip in my mind about Throckmorton's knowledge of ponds and lakes, but thought better of trotting it out. Instead, I continued undeterred, "That may well be. But I've explained to Chris that he has a right to call anybody he wants in his defense, nevertheless. And the honors case might also concern your position here, what with all those students giving testimony. Just a word to the wise."

"Get out of my office!"

"By the way," I gave one last parting shot, "I'll try to overlook the slur on my ethnic heritage." I exited to the sound of the office door closing behind me with a vehement bump. They dropped the case against Chris the next week for lack of evidence. Just like cats, frogs don't want to be skinned to reveal their ugly innards.

Chris brought the news to me at home, elated, "Thank you so much, Nick. I don't know how . . . "

"Nothing to thank. It's only fair. But we need to discuss something else. Go listen to the answering machine in the office." When I had returned home that afternoon, a message on the tape ran, "Chris. If you want to rent the basement apartment starting this summer, please let me know." When Chris came back, he started to explain, but I cut him off, "It's all right. We haven't been happy recently living together, and I know the late nights and the letters all point to the same conclusion: I think you should take the apartment."

"You read my letters, you asshole!" he shouted.

"I didn't need to," I replied quietly. "But I'd like to know just one thing: where have you been meeting this man?"

"More like men. In the library. We usually park down by the lake." And he added as if it were perfectly reasonable, "I'd like to stay. We could turn the office back into a second bedroom."

"So you could bring your tricks back to do it here instead of in the backseat of a car? No, I think you need to move out. We have a better chance of surviving our last few weeks in relative peace that way. It's clear to me that you're just not ready to settle down." At this he grabbed his car keys and left the apartment, grim-faced. I didn't even break down—until he had slammed the door behind him.

Separations don't happen suddenly or completely; they progress in slow motion, prolonging the dull ache. We weren't cross with one another on a daily basis; in fact, we adopted a curious deference. With the matter apparently settled, Chris still came to church with me, still came home for dinner, and still slept with me, odd to say, though without any sex.

Eventually we had to agree on some division of the apartment's contents. I assumed he would take the furniture and decorations he had scattered around the place. "Do you want some help moving your belongings," I asked as we approached exam week.

"I can take the clothes on my own in the station wagon. The furniture stays here," he replied.

"Most of it's yours."

"Well, my new place is furnished, and anyhow, all this stuff was a gift. I don't really need it. You do, since I removed your old junk. I don't take gifts back."

"That's really generous," I puzzled, "But I can always buy new things."

"Look, I want you to have it," he said charitably, followed by, "Maybe it would be better if I stayed?" Did this represent a half-hearted plea for reconciliation or just for my acquiescence to his infidelity? It contained no element of apology or any hint of giving up his random partners. But I should have begged that question and asked whether he truly loved me enough to change. Instead, I gave an instant reply that I'll regret for the rest of my life: "Given this semester, I don't think that'd be a good idea. Even if we lived as housemates, I'd have expectations of something more, and that would just make for more conflict. You move out. We might even remain friends that way."

He shouted with sudden and surprising bitterness, "Friends? You must be joking. To be honest, I don't want the stuff because it'll remind me of you!"

We finished the last days of exams in a bleak, determined silence. But watching Chris drive sullenly away filled me with a sorrow that reached into my very soul. And I came to understand heartbreak not as a figure of speech but as a physical affliction.

I felt that a love I had prized more deeply than anything else in the world had slipped out of reach, its solace ebbing away like my life's blood into the desiccating sands of irrevocable estrangement. Perhaps I should have recalled a different bit of wisdom from Hofmannsthal when Chris and I first met: "To hold and embrace, to hold and then let go. Life punishes those who cannot do this, and God—God has no mercy on them."

> Lost is my quiet for ever,
> Lost is life's happiest part;
> Lost all my fruitless endeavors
> To touch an inimical heart.
>
> But tho' my despair is past curing,
> And much undeserv'd is my fate,
> I'll show by a patient enduring
> That I shall not yield to his hate.

13 COME TO THE CABARET

The shock of my predictable existence splintering into shards ran so deep that events seemed to move in slow motion, and I continued my chores more out of habit than purpose. Eventually, I tried to fashion a new life for myself, and I noticed that Chris deliberately avoided places he thought I might frequent. Mutual gay friends related his tales of my terrible behavior, how I bullied him out of our apartment. I didn't defend myself, because I felt like the man in court asked, "When did you stop beating your boyfriend?" I knew the truth: I had contributed my share of animosity as our relationship fell apart. But we had enjoyed each other's company until that last semester, and even at the end I wasn't the monster he now described. In fact, I had saved his graduate-student career. But I kept entirely silent on that score, as I did about his frequent infidelities—these were widely known.

As far as my work was concerned, I should have relaxed after attaining the ultimate job security. But Little Boy Blue tried continually to make my life unpleasant, and slowly but surely I began to regard tenure as a life sentence rather than as a release from uncertainty. Still, I could speak my mind freely now, and when my antagonist contradicted me rudely in front of the faculty gathered for a meeting, I addressed him quite plainly, "There are some people in this room who don't pull their weight, and I don't need to take mediocrity seriously." As we left the meeting, Little Boy tried to back me into a corner of the room with a menacing sneer, "You need to shut up, Walker, or we'll do to you what we should have done when you arrived."

The threat of violence made me laugh, "You'll need a lot higher set of elevator shoes for that, or maybe you can hire some of your rougher New York trade to do the job."

He became livid and went to see the Dean. I duly received a summons, "It's not going to help you here, Professor Walker, if you talk about mediocrity in faculty meetings. I've received complaints. Around here we have a motto: 'to get along, go along.'"

"I know who complained. How about a different motto, 'What goes around comes around?' Let me point out that it's not going to serve a good many people here (I left 'present company included' unspoken but understood), if I start revealing things that go on behind closet doors." Instead of retribution, this impudent retort gained me a semester's leave and a stipend for research abroad funded by a German government agency in an exchange agreement with the University. The Pulpitville way involved moving troublemakers off campus and out of sight.

For the remainder of the fall semester I fell back on dating men I had known before I met Chris. I called sweet Keith, the pharmacist of yore, who still had his amazing boa constrictor in shape. We tried a month of sleeping over and having unsatisfactory sex. Such a nice man, so well-mannered, a bit boring, and totally incompatible for all his intelligence, pleasant looks, and entirely too ample equipment. "This isn't going to work, is it," he finally commented, more resigned than disappointed.

"No, it's not. I'd like to be able to take advantage of everything you have to offer, which is a lot. But we'd always be two pitchers in search of a catcher." He flashed his bashful smile, and I never saw him again.

I made an appointment with Jason to have my hair cut, with the predictable result that he wound up bent over the shampoo sink in the back of his shop after he had closed. He immediately entangled me in the quite comfortable domestic life of weekends at his place, dinners out, and clubbing, where I saw Chris for the first time in a couple of months. When he spotted me, he practically ran out of the place. Upset, I exited too, which Jason took calmly. After some wonderful sex when we arrived back in his bedroom, he asked to hear my account of the affair. He listened patiently as I babbled on, then offered, "You're still stuck on that guy, aren't you, Nick?"

I looked straight into his beautiful blue eyes, "No. Done with that one."

"I don't think so, sugar," came Jason's sage reply. "Don't get me wrong—having you sleep beside me again is great. But as long as the sight of Chris upsets you, you're tied to him. I saw you looking at him, staring really, even while dancing with me. I don't pay that no never mind. It's just how it goes, and you should come to grips with it."

"Sorry, didn't mean to be rude."

"No harm done. But I can tell you why we can't go on with this: you'd compare me to him constantly. Now turn out the light and go to sleep. I guess I can catch you on the rebound for one more night. Besides, you're too sexy, and I might could say too 'nice,' to throw out in the middle of the night."

Of course Jason spoke wisely. The sight of Chris upset me because I still had feelings for him on some level I couldn't reach. And so, in the classic manner of characters in nineteenth-century novels, I put my failed love affair behind me during a tour abroad. I retreated to Berlin for a couple of months, leaving my apartment in the care of a student house sitter.

Until now I haven't spoken much of Berlin, where I had spent nine months of my graduate-student year overseas researching in its multitude of library collections divided between East and West. For me it was and will always remain the fabled city of Christopher Isherwood's short stories about the late 1920s and early 30s, tales on which the musical and movie *Cabaret* were based. Most of the city's buildings from that era had vanished, bombed into rubble by Allied forces at the end of World War II. Yet its sardonically hedonistic soul survived the decades-long occupation (and still thrives today in the gleaming new metropolis).

West Berlin, where Americans lived in the mid 80s, assumed an air of a luxurious ocean liner impounded in a foreign port, surrounded on all sides by hostile authorities. Conscious of their precarious berth, the passengers gave themselves over to a permissive style of life that careened from amusement to amusement at a frenzied pace twenty-four hours a day. They gambled, drank, and fornicated with abandon, as if port police might storm the ship at any moment, taking all into custody. *Carpe diem* didn't begin to describe the intensity with which Berliners lived. They worked hard (and in this way the inhabitants reminded me a bit of Chicagoans) but they played twice as hard (like New Yorkers). It was a glorious, freewheeling place, packed with foreign soldiers (French, British, American) and Germans who liked living on the edge with a certain fatalistic nonchalance amid a kaleidoscope of pleasure.

Western overindulgence contrasted starkly with the cynical asceticism of the East in all its repressive puritanism (reinforced by Russian troops). "Our People, Our Solidarity, Our Socialist Democracy" shouted red banners hanging insincerely from many of the official buildings, most of which had not been entirely repaired since the last war. Bullet holes still showed in the stonework of the Prussian State Library on Unter den Linden, the main avenue in a city center trapped behind the wall that separated East from West.

Political dissonance exuded from a populace that could hear the Western version of the news at 6 PM and then the Eastern version at 6:30. Spies lurked everywhere, especially in East Berlin, and one took care to avoid interrogation by the VoPo ("People's Police," who detained me anyhow on one occasion) or, worse, by the Stasi (State Security Service), which enlisted legions of informers to watch over the populace. Negotiating Berlin became at once a trial and a sport, and I traveled many days from West to East across the border to do my research and take in the incongruous glories of the city.

During the winter Berlin turned unfathomably dark and cold, with a wan daylight occasionally suffusing the grey overcast. The German exchange service found me a neat modern one-bedroom apartment on Waitzstraße, not far from the Lehniner Platz subway stop and the main commercial boulevard in the West, the Kurfürstendamm. Using the subway I could travel all over the city for my work and recreation (the center of the commercial area had many gay bars where one could take refuge from the gloom in the company of one's fellows).

From my former visits I knew my way around the watering holes, and during my second week there on a dreary Friday night dusted by snow flurries, the very pavement frigidly aching, I sought out the nearest gay locale. I sat in the only open seat at the bar, next to a man sporting a military haircut, He dressed in a leather bomber jacket left open to reveal a blue button-down with tee shirt underneath and casual slacks. (No, I didn't forget you were listening; and yes, I still had a weakness for military men. So arrest me, already.) He had medium brown hair matching his eyes and the kind of regular good looks that could only fit, in light of his clothes, an American. He remained very quiet, I would almost say withdrawn, but he kept giving me sidelong glances when he thought I wasn't looking. And after I ordered a drink, he struck up a conversation with a simple question, "*Italiener?*"

"*Nee, Amerikaner wie du.*"

"Really? Your German is excellent," he reverted to American.

"Thank my mother. She grew up in a German-speaking province of northern Italy. My turn: Army? Hmmm, officer I would guess. Captain, maybe?"

"Do I *look* Army?" He glanced at himself in the mirror behind the bar and seemed a little put out, "What gave me away?"

"Well, the haircut for the military part. For the officer appraisal: enlisted men don't usually dress in prep-school khakis. And you strike me as a little too mature for a lieutenant."

"Major, actually. Scott, Scott Willemer." He extended his substantial mitt; he was a tall man, maybe 6'2.

"Nice to meet you Scott, Scott (he suppressed a wry grin). Nick Walker," I shook hands.

He hesitated for a second, then inquired tentatively, "Tourist?"

"No, college professor of German history on a research leave, sheltering from the cold lonely night."

"So you don't subscribe to Philina's view?"

"Philina?"

"A German history prof. should know Goethe's *Wilhelm Meister*. I'm beginning to think you're an imposter, but maybe you forgot (he recited in German):

> Sing not thus in tones of sadness
> Of the loneliness of night;
> No! 'tis made for social gladness,
> Converse sweet and love's delight.

> Who can hail the day with pleasure
> Which but interrupts our joys,
> Keeps us from our dreams of leisure
> With its glare and irksome noise?

> But when night is come and glowing
> With the lamp's attemper'd ray,
> And from lip to lip are flowing
> Love and mirth in sparkling play;

> Then, my lad, this comfort borrow
> In the long day's lingering light:
> Ev'ry day hath its own sorrow,
> Gladness cometh with the night.

"Okay, you get the prize for the all-time weirdest pickup routine I've ever heard. Does that work?"

"We're gonna find out. But just in case, let me try something more conventional: could I buy you a round of whatever you're drinking?"

"Johnny Walker Black with a splash."

He smiled a little in spite of himself and then added, "No cheap date."

"Who said anything about a date?"

He looked sheepish and became very reserved again, "Sorry. Didn't mean it exactly that way."

"*Kein Problem*. Anyhow, I really don't know anybody in town."

"I know lots of people in town, but this place is off limits and . . . " he hesitated.

"It's full of servicemen."

"None of whom I can . . . " he stopped again, and I wondered what made this large handsome man so reticent.

"I'm not off limits, at least the last time I looked."

"You probably are, but I guess that's why I'm here. So are you gonna stay and help me drink tonight? It's nice to meet somebody outside the service for a change."

"I'm not only going to stay, I'll buy the next round. I need to confess, though, I have a thing for military men. . . . "

"Don't stop now."

"Tell you some other time. So where did you learn German?"

"I've been posted at various bases in Germany during my service, and there's a bit of family background too. I'm actually taking a master's in German at the Freie Universität. Out in Dahlem, near our base?"

"And thus your literary bent. Be careful—somebody might mistake you for an academic type."

"I'll take that as a compliment. In fact, I'm going back to the states in the summer to teach."

"Where?"

"West Point. The Army sent me here to get the degree, and then I'll do a three-year faculty stint there."

I noticed then that he wore a heavy gold class ring inset with a black star sapphire.

"Graduate of West Point?"

"Yes sir," he answered very formally. "Do you work here?"

"I'm nominally attached to the Technische Universität—over by the Zoo Station? (He knew the location.) But I teach at Pulpitville."

"Big-time university!" He became more congenial and relaxed as the alcohol overcame his inhibitions.

"So they say, Major. I'm not so sure. But I can pull rank too: I have tenure and students call me Professor Walker, but you can call me Professor Nick."

This time he actually managed to laugh and kept chatting through another three rounds, when he started zipping up his jacket, "Well, time to go."

"I suppose you're going to crawl to the next bar?"

"Actually, I have two choices. I can go back to the base and officers' quarters, or an extremely good looking, somewhat drunk, quite personable college professor might possibly invite me back to his place for a nightcap. I have a weekend pass."

"I expected better than the 'I'm-recalled-to-barracks-on-Monday-and-only-have-a-few-hours-left' routine. I've heard that one before. But I just might find a place for a 'somewhat drunk' well-built Army major in my living room"—he frowned—"maybe for a chat"—he frowned a little more deeply—"Oh, come on, Scott, let's go to my apartment. I guess I can stand some company, just to ward off the cold and keep up the morale of our fighting men stationed overseas. You can sleep on the sofa"—his face didn't exactly become a picture of grief, but keen disappointment showed—"or maybe a more comfortable 'rack.'"

"Just sleep?"

"And the hits just keep on coming. At ease, Major. I must say, you really seemed shy at first, but when you make up your mind, you don't hold back."

"Sometimes when you see an objective you want to take, you need to move quickly to maintain the element of surprise." He blushed.

"Good tactics. Okay, we head for the subway station on the corner, and I'm about four stops up the Ku'damm."

"Yes sir, Professor Nick, sir," he let a grin slip out at this.

"Okay, you can knock it off. We're in an informal social surrounding, if you hadn't noticed."

"Yes sir . . . I mean Nick, sir." Irrepressibility scored a definite point in his favor.

When we arrived back at my building, I punched the button that lit the stairwell for all of 30 seconds, and we raced up a two flights to see who could get there first. I won.

"Out of shape, Major? I should've found a marine."

"Want me to break your face?"

"Not especially."

He apologized, "Just kiddin'."

"Me too. Army boy for me every time: you probably let me beat you."

"That's it!"

"Need another drink?"

"Sure, that'd be great." And as I retrieved a couple of glasses from the small kitchen and an open bottle of wine, I noticed that my new companion was still examining me as carefully as he had in the bar. This scrutiny, though subtle, assumed an unusual air. We chatted for a while, until I finally decided to move things along, partly to escape the somewhat disconcerting inspection, "I'm going to turn in."

"Thought you'd never ask. I'm ready for action."

"I don't recall inviting you—as I said, the sofa works just fine." His downcast glance melted my resolve, which was very meager by that time, and I allowed, "Oh, all right. But I'm a light sleeper, so you'd better not snore."

"Then we'll need to stay awake all night."

Scott wasn't exactly a beginner, and for a big man he moved very gently and gradually. We kissed on the sofa until we couldn't stand it any more, and then started to strip off one another's clothes (my favorite part). We made for the bedroom to go completely naked, and I liked what I saw: he wasn't muscle-bound or flabby, just solid—a nice chest lightly dusted by short brown hair, the trail running down to that wonderful fullness below the waist.

He liked what he saw too, and let me know, "Wow, the body's as beautiful as the face!" But when I tried to start, he said, "Whoa, trooper. Totally safe. Have you been tested? (I hadn't; it had just become available.)

Then let's play without any real sex. I know it's frustrating."

"Have *you* been tested?"

"Every three months. I'd like you to get tested too. It takes about two weeks to receive the results, but if it comes back negative and you don't see any other guys, we can do more."

"No rush. But you're making me feel like a teenager—you mean you want to go 'steady'?"

"I know a good thing when I see it," and then he colored, not having realized how I could take that. He started to explain, "I mean . . . I like you . . ."

"Don't worry—I like the whole package too. Stay the weekend and we can find out whether we can get along for more than an evening."

"Do you always invite strange men to spend the weekend."

"You invited yourself, and I admit you are 'strange'—well, make that ' unusual.'"

"I'll spend all weekend working out whether that's a compliment. I'd need to go back to base for a change of clothes. But yeah, sounds like a plan." He hesitated again, unsure, "It's been a very long time."

Usually men boast of their sexual prowess, and his honesty charmed me, "Don't worry. I don't expect an earthquake on the first 'date.'" We had to shower after we finished.

After we awoke in the late morning, he went back to his base to retrieve fresh clothes and an overnight bag. When he returned Saturday afternoon, we became better acquainted. Scott was about two years older than I. He had grown up in Nebraska in a large ranching family that immigrated two generations before from Hannover. He wanted to break free, and his father had some pull, arranging admission to West Point. After graduation Scott went straight to Vietnam as a second lieutenant in charge of an infantry squad, then a platoon, and by the beginning of his second tour he had been promoted to first lieutenant commanding a company ("I've seen enough combat to last me a whole lifetime"—he had long scar running down the inside length of his thigh as proof that didn't bear questioning).

Following his extended tour in Vietnam, Scott explained, he rose to the rank of captain, and finally, after some time in Wiesbaden and Kaiserslautern, a major. The Army didn't select him for General Staff School, a sign that he'd probably retire as a lieutenant colonel. His aptitude for German came partly from hearing it spoken by his grandmother, partly from a real talent for foreign languages. He related the events of his life slowly, almost reluctantly. And there was something else: a mysterious air of melancholy beneath his calm surface.

Despite being taciturn and overly serious at times, Scott possessed an easy way with people. He was unexpectedly sensitive and quietly assured. We spent the remainder of my time in Berlin together when he was free—occasionally evenings for dinner, whole weekends when he had a pass. This ritual reminded me of my initial encounter with Chris in its abrupt beginning, but it continued in a more relaxed way.

Knowing that shared experience cements friendships, I proposed a kind of tour, "Have you explored the city, Scott? It has a remarkable history, prewar as well as postwar."

"Not really. I suppose I hang around the base too much or in the American sector with other officers."

"Then let me show you the sights. I spent two semesters here as a student looking for all the historic spots, official and otherwise. Can Army personnel cross the border?"

"Actually, it's called crossing into another 'sector,' and yeah, I have free access to all of them."

"Then let's see the sights."

We toured all the places that I had discovered during my student years with Isherwood for my guide and a quite a few more. For me this represented nostalgia, for Scott novelty. We roamed the whole city from the Alexander Platz in the east to the Olympic Stadium in the West, where Hitler had presided over the games in 1936. The remnants of Sachsenhausen, the first Nazi concentration camp for "undesirables"—communists, dissidents, dissenting journalists, Jews, homosexuals among them—moved Scott most deeply. Not to be outdone, the Soviets had then used the facility as an internment camp for political prisoners and German prisoners of war housed in horrible conditions. "Ever notice how much extreme ideologies resemble each other? You know that officially there aren't any gay people in East Germany. If they even suspect somebody, they arrest them." I wondered whether he applied that thought to his own situation in the military.

On weekend evenings we searched for (and found) various gay bars, had dinners out, and made love. In those several weeks I realized what my two years with Chris had failed to teach me: that Pulpitville would always immure me in a post-adolescent world. The dangerously alluring students never grew old, though the faces changed. I needed a constant, responsible man to anchor my life: Scott held the promise of adult stability and also offered a mature physical attraction.

He seemed very interested about what attracted me to military men. And I finally related the *South Pacific* episode and my first puppy love with Wes.

"Enlisted man, huh?" he commented somewhat oddly, then added, "So, had a thing for guys in uniform from the beginning?"

"To invoke the patois of the Army: 'Fuckin' A,'" I replied, "Literally!"

"That's pathetic," he groaned, "The one time you use slang, professor, you make a bad pun!"

"It was a *little* funny," which brought back his gentle smile.

I also told him about the grad students, the undergrads, and Chris.

"Ah, a lot of young guys and another man!"

"You think I'm depraved."

"Nah. I think I should've have had more fun along the way."

"Don't worry. The 'other man' is history now. Confess, Major. Any troopers in your past?"

He evaded the question, "Dating other soldiers is dangerous. *You* won't get in trouble for having an affair with another guy. If they find out about *me*, they'll hand out a dishonorable discharge." He would relate nothing further about specific affairs. But I came to have a real affection for him and to understand that he took our brief encounter very seriously when he started asking whether I planned to stay in Tennelina.

"I've been looking to leave since day one. It's a good position, but I can't stand small-town life, the location, or the university, to tell the truth. And it's not getting better. But I don't know when I can leave or where I'll go. You?"

"I'll enjoy the posting at West Point, kind of a homecoming. But after that, I have just a year before I can retire. I'm not going career Army; I've done my service, and I can't live this way, constantly hiding who I am. It makes me unhappy, and I don't just mean being constantly loaded for bear with all the targets off limits. I mean concealing my feelings, not sharing my joys and disappointments when all the other guys talk about their girlfriends and wives. By the way, the men on base here all think I'm going with some Berlin girl on my weekends off."

I glanced downward, "Wrong equipment, Major."

"And I wouldn't have it any other way!"

All good things must come to an end, I knew, though I was reluctant to depart. I didn't recognize the full extent of his regret about our separation until the night before I left. We spent our last Saturday together, finishing with an elaborate dinner at the restaurant in the Bristol-Kempinski, just then the most fashionable place in the city. My train was to leave the Zoo Station at 11 AM on Sunday morning, and we would have one more night. When we returned from dinner, Scott became very earnest, "Nick, I'd like this not to end; I'd like to see you again."

"Feeling's mutual, but how would that work?"

"I get my degree in May, and then I have a couple of weeks do anything else I want before I report to West Point. What if I were to visit you in Pulpitville?"

"You'd be welcome. I really don't want our time to become just one more page in my scrapbook."

A Chosen Landscape

"You keep a scrapbook?"

"Of course not. I mean that I want to keep seeing you. Otherwise I'll find myself looking at a photograph a couple of years from now and wonder what might have been."

"Then I have a plan: after I visit you in Pulpitville, you visit me at West Point."

"They allow that?"

"Yeah, there are some rooms for guests on post. I'll just bill you as an expert in German history I met in Berlin, all true."

"You've made a deal. Now let's catch some time between the sheets tonight, because we won't be able to do anything but shake hands at the station."

Scott intrigued me in the unusual combination of his striking physicality and intelligence. As the train eased slowly out of the Bahnhof am Zoo, I foresaw prospects of adventure at least, and at most the hope of that stable adult existence for which I had searched without success in Pulpitville.

14 TIES THAT BIND

Future prospects never unfold quite as we imagine, and mine held an unexpected and extremely painful episode. As soon as I arrived back in Pulpitville, during that time usually spent readjusting after a long absence, I received a phone call that filled me with dread. Across the line I heard a woman's voice, just vaguely familiar in its reserved upper-class East-Coast accent, "Is this Professor Walker?"

"Speaking."

"I don't know if you remember me, but this is Joan Caldwell—Christopher's mother."

When she gave her name, the memories flooded back, of our cryptic conversation during Christmas break over three years before, of messages left on our answering machine when Chris and I lived together, of the hope at the beginning of our relationship and the disappointment at its bitter end. What could possibly prompt her to call me? I tried not to let anxiety enter my voice, "Mrs. Caldwell, yes, I remember. What can I do for you?"

"I'm here in town. Might we lunch some day very soon?"

"Certainly. When would be convenient? I'm on research leave, and I don't have any fixed schedule."

"Are you free today? 12:30 at the Fin and Feather?"

"That'd be fine."

A million alarming things ran through my mind. Did she know this was the first place Chris had taken me to? Would she inquire about our living together, whether her son had been more than just my roommate? Having discovered the nature of our relationship, would she inform the University, asking for me to be dismissed for turpitude? Or would she just deliver a stern and disapproving lecture? I had no idea, but her tone seemed urgent and distressed.

When I arrived at that sedate restaurant, I beheld a woman sitting at a secluded window table, gazing distractedly out over the same courtyard Chris and I had first viewed several years earlier. She dressed with an elegant simplicity that bespoke wealth, and she obviously had enjoyed uncommon beauty in her youth: her face still bore a faded loveliness. Her neatly and somewhat severely coiffed hair was auburn like Chris's, though lighter, as if she had once been blond. And she had clearly authored his bright blue eyes. But she wore a drawn expression now, as if time or circumstance had burdened her with unanticipated cares.

She did not rise but politely extended her hand, which I shook.

She began, "It's good to meet you. Shall we order? Would you like a glass of wine?"

"Yes, I would."

As we waited for the drinks, she began with a question, "How long has it been since you've seen my son?"

"Quite some time, actually. After he moved out a year ago, we didn't stay on good terms. And recently I've been in Germany for several months. How did you know I was a professor?"

"When I arrived in Pulpitville, I looked you up in the University directory. And then I called your department to see if you were there, but they told me you had traveled abroad."

Called the department? I thought with alarm.

"I, really we, tried very hard to locate you." She must have seen the look of concern in my reaction, "Oh, but I haven't yet related the reason for contacting you. I don't wish to seem mysterious: Christopher has been taken very ill. His older brother and sister are here too."

"His father?"

"Christopher's father has advanced Alzheimer's disease. He lives in an adult care facility now."

"How is Chris doing?"

"Not well, I'm afraid. Christopher came down with a severe case of meningitis and collapsed in his apartment last weekend. He's in the intensive care unit of the hospital, unconscious."

"I'm extremely sorry to hear that." Then I continued reluctantly, "Does he have AIDS?"

"No, Professor Walker—may I call you Nicholas? (I nodded)—he tested negative. But his meningitis caused brain swelling and severe damage."

"Did you know that Chris and I, that we were, well, lovers?"

"It wasn't very hard to figure out at the time, really. Two men living together, the one keeping house and buying furniture, the other cooking, vacationing together. And for a long time he could talk of nothing but you, your intelligence, your accomplishments. Knowing Chris's penchant of beautiful things, I didn't need him to tell me about your looks. (I may have colored.) I had suspected Christopher was gay from the time he went off to college. I actually rejoiced to know he had settled down; he's always been a somewhat unpredictable boy," she paused to correct, ". . . man, and even though we had no idea about your age, you seemed to create some firm center to his life. Eventually, too, he related the story of his honors violation. Did you play a role in having it dismissed?"

"Yes, I had some special leverage. It concerned the people who brought the charges and their motivation. He felt—I did too—that it had something to do with our living arrangement. It turned out that his first roommate and a faculty member, well, let's just say, harbored some personal malice toward Chris."

"I had no idea it was so unsavory as that," Mrs. Caldwell replied.

"Unfortunately, yes. But that also made it easy to deflect."

"Thank you for your help," she continued, "My instincts about you ran true, then. When Christopher told me he was moving out, I encouraged him to stay. I hoped you might be able to watch out for him."

"The separation came very hard for me, more so for him. But Chris simply wasn't ready to settle down with one person. And in the present climate, you'll excuse me, I considered that dangerous."

The server brought our meal and we paused to eat in silence, until she asked another question that seemed very important to her, "Are you still in love with my son?"

"I'll always love him," I declared immediately, then paused to think how best to continue. "On some deep level Chris has marked my life permanently with a special sense of worth. I can't simply forget living with him for all that time, and I'll always cherish the memory of the wonderful experiences we enjoyed. But we didn't part amicably. If you had asked me a year ago, I might have imagined reconciliation as an outside chance after the initial anger had passed. But time intervened, and we both moved on. I'm sorry."

"Don't apologize. I can understand that. But I still have a favor to ask. Would you visit him in the hospital? He won't know you're there, but it would make me . . . it would make us feel better. You're the only other person he's ever known so thoroughly, aside from his immediate family."

I tried to conquer the intense feeling of regret that suddenly threatened to overwhelm me, "Of course I'd see him. Anything I can do."

She seemed very relieved at this answer, "Thank you so much, Nicholas. Can you come with me after lunch?" She signaled for the check.

"That'd be fine."

She ushered me to her Mercedes for the ride to the hospital, where the scene was far grimmer than I had imagined. A nurse signed us in and then conducted us back to a private room in the ICU. There Chris's brother, Robert, and sister, Lisa, awaited me and his mother. Robert took over. "Thanks for coming," he said in a subdued voice, "I'm Rob," and he reached out to shake hands. Chris lay immobile, attached to countless monitors, an IV, and a ventilator that rose and fell methodically, breathing for him. His face was haggard, his skin gray; he had lost an incredible amount of weight for somebody already slender.

I stood motionless for a while, and then asked, "May I touch him?" His mother murmured her assent and I grasped his right hand, remembering how many times I had held it in the car, in the theater, at home. It possessed less warmth now, and the fine bones stood in stark relief through the pale skin. I released, "Do you want me to stay?"

"Please. And come as you often as you wish. We're hoping he'll wake up soon," Rob offered faintly as if he held no such hope. He drove me back to my car in the restaurant parking lot, asking a bit of how I came to know Chris but probing no further.

Nine days passed like an eternity, with me shuttling repeatedly back and forth to the hospital, trying to focus on organizing my research, awaiting Scott's arrival on a Friday. I talked with Chris's brother and sister, mostly his brother, about Chris's childhood and adolescence, "My mother cares especially about Chris. He was born with some terrible intestinal defect and had multiple surgeries as an infant. That may explain why he didn't grow very tall. But as a kid he was always the family wit, always the one to crack a smile. And I wanted him to enjoy college, so as a present for his twenty-first birthday I wrote him a large check with a memo: 'for drugs, sex, and rock 'n' roll.' Mother was not amused. Did you guys have fun?"

"We certainly did until we broke up—a hard decision for both of us, and we didn't handle it well." I couldn't think of what more I might tell him, "He could really make me laugh too, and he always teased me about being a pompous college professor, something very refreshing, actually. But he just couldn't adapt to exclusive domestic life. And then there was trouble at school for him and with my department for me. Bad timing. Do you really think he'll recover?"

"No. We're waiting—waiting for my mother to make her mind up to let him go. But while the machines grind away, I suppose a small part of me maintains some unrealistic notion that I'll walk into the room and he'll just miraculously open his eyes and scold, 'So don't just stand around, all of you. Do something, make yourselves useful. I'm hungry and it's too cold in here.'"

I looked down at the floor, "Sounds about right."

The morning of Scott's arrival I went to the hospital, and Rob took me aside, "This afternoon . . . you see the damage to his brain was just too . . . ." He looked weary and hollow, and he didn't need to supply the rest of the thought he couldn't utter anyhow. They intended to remove life support.

"Do you want me here—I have a friend flying in, and I need to pick him up at the airport."

"Let me ask Mother." He came back, "We'll wait for you, if you wish."

"I'll return in a couple of hours, as soon as I drop my guest at my apartment."

When Scott stepped out of the jetway into the terminal, he presented a magnificent sight in his Army green service uniform with a good many ribbons and golden oak leaves on his shoulders. He smiled at me, we shook hands, and he gave a quiet aside, "You said you like guys in uniforms, no?"

"Definitely! All of them (he frowned a little) and a particular major I know. You're spectacular. Are you one of those major majors?"

He let a faint smile emerge at the ribbing, "And it gets me a discount on the airfare too. No luggage except the suit bag and overnight case . . . they shipped most of my stuff to West Point."

When we reached the car I explained, "I going to leave you at the apartment for a while. Is that all right? There's something I need to do."

"What? You look upset, Nick."

"It's Chris. His family's in town, and they want me to visit him in the hospital."

Scott sounded more than a little distressed, wondering, no doubt, if he had made a pointless detour to see me, "I hoped, well, that the field was clear, so to speak. I thought our time in Berlin . . . that it was special."

"Flattery will get you anything. It *was* special, and you are." Then I clarified, "Nothing's changed there. Chris is in intensive care with meningitis. They want me to stop by." I didn't supply the details.

He shook his head, "Not good. It happens to soldiers sometimes, especially young recruits in barracks during basic. Don't worry about me. I had to change planes in Chicago, so it's been a long trip. I need a nap anyhow." I dropped him at my place, showed him where he could put his clothes, and by the time I left, he was sound asleep on my sofa, a talent he had developed in the service for dozing on a moment's notice.

When I arrived at the ICU, Chris's mother, sister, and brother were waiting. That family clearly didn't shed tears in public, and Joan Caldwell in particular had set her face in grim resignation. They had said their farewells before I arrived.

"May I say goodbye?" I asked quietly. Chris's mother agreed. I brushed my fingers over the delicate hair on the back of his right hand, then entwined my fingers in his, leaned over and whispered very close to his ear, "Go easy, my friend," and kissed him gently on the forehead.

His family stood on one side, his mother holding his hand, I stood on the other, my hand on his shoulder as the nurse disconnected all the sensors on his now sunken chest, removed the oxygen monitor, turned off all the alarms on the machines, and pulled his breathing tube. He took a couple of short reflexive breaths, then went still. After a short pause Rob asked the resident when Chris's heart would stop beating. It already had, the earnest young man with a stethoscope informed us. Everything had happened in a few minutes. I nodded a resigned goodbye to the Caldwells, because I didn't think I could retain my composure any longer, and left the room. But Rob followed me down the corridor, "Wait, Professor Walker—Nick. My mother wants me to thank you for coming."

In my shock I only thought to say, "Will there be services? Would I be welcome?"

"I'll need to ask her, but I think so. We'll be in touch about the arrangements. We have a guest cottage on the estate. I'm sure if I suggested it to my mother, you could stay there if you attended."

When I walked in the door of my apartment, Scott perched on the sofa, dressed in carefully pressed civilian clothes now, button-down shirt and creased slacks, just as when I had first met him in Berlin. He glanced up from the magazine he was reading and only needed one look to know what had happened, "He didn't make it." I shook my head no. "I'm so sorry, Nick." I sat down next to him, entirely mute. He thought for a moment, and then in his calm way added, "I've seen this, I mean young men from my company in Vietnam dying. As their commanding officer, I couldn't afford the luxury of tears. But I used to tell my men that there's no dishonor, nothing unmanly in crying at the loss of a fallen friend." At that I buried my face in his broad shoulder and wept until I was spent. He just wrapped his arm over my back, rubbing it gently, persistently to soothe me.

Finally I said something mundane and ridiculous, "I've ruined your shirt."

"It'll dry out, Nick."

"If I hadn't let Chris go, move out, he'd be alive now. I needed to be there for him."

"How do you figure that?" Scott assessed quietly. "You're away on a research grant for a semester, he comes home alone on a weekend night after partying with his friends. He starts feeling ill on Saturday morning, thinks it's just flu. Goes to bed with a headache, gets up in the middle of the night and collapses. His department doesn't realize something's wrong until Monday, when he's due in class. Same result. Nothing you could do. It was just his time."

"Too early."

"It's always too early for guys that age," he replied glumly. He started to tell me about his experience during the war, then he hesitated and thought better of it, "What do you want now? Do you need to go back to the family? (I shook my head no.) Should we get some dinner? Go out or order in?"

"I think I'd like to eat at a nice place I know in town. Nothing too fancy, but they have a good bar. I really need a drink."

"Or three. And some food—you need to get something in you. You look wrung out, trooper."

On the way to the restaurant, driving through town, an old car in the lane next to us backfired loudly, and suddenly Scott dove for the well in front of the passenger seat. It came reflexively and instantly, and when he emerged from the ball into which he had gathered himself, he looked ashen for a moment. He peered out the window nervously at his surroundings, then turned to me with a sheepish smile, "Just taking cover. Sometimes . . . ."

I cut him off, "You don't need to explain."

When we reached the restaurant, they didn't have a table right away, and we sat drinking at the bar. Finally seated, I needed a change of subject and asked him whether had visited his family in Nebraska.

"Yeah, for a couple of days. My folks were happy to see me, I guess, and my brother and sister. There was a reception, the neighbors came and some friends from high school who still live there."

"Do your parents know, I mean about . . ."

"No, of course not. They just keep asking why I'm not married at 38. It gets old. You'd think they'd figure it out, and anyhow, they have three grandchildren."

"So you didn't tell them about your brilliant, charming, handsome boyfriend?" I kidded, and for the first time that evening we laughed.

"Yeah, right. 'By the way, folks, I'm gay, I'm seeing this overly modest college professor, and I'm going off to teach at West Point. Don't let anybody else know.'"

"They're going to find out if one or the other of us gets pregnant. You'd need to make an honest man out of me."

"Sure, we can keep working on those items. Do *your* parents know?"

"About me? Certainly. And my mother, at least, guessed about Chris, though she never met him. She didn't exactly approve at first, but it wasn't up to her. My father's never brought up the subject, which means he has no objections. I bet they'd like you."

"How so?"

"My father held the rank of captain in the Army during World War II."

"Infantry?"

"OSS."

"Espionage?" Scott exclaimed.

"I guess, although they liked to call it 'intelligence.' He won't tell me much; I think he made some dangerous trips from Lugano in Switzerland to Como in Italy, running a resistance network at the end of the war. He met my mother there."

"He must be a brave guy."

"He doesn't describe it that way. He's quiet and thoughtful and very bright. His job was to blend in, not stand out. He's rather like you, calm and controlled. Look, I need to go home. I'm exhausted."

Scott understood perfectly, picked up the check to my protests, which he ignored, "I'm a guest at your place. It's the least I can do."

When we returned to the apartment, he offered to sleep in the guest bedroom. "Absolutely not!" I insisted, "I don't want to be alone tonight. But I'm not really very . . . I mean . . . can you just hold me? I know you must be eager, but I just don't think I'd be very good."

"We're playing it your way, professor."

But the night was neither peaceful nor comforting. Scott slept restlessly, had a terrible nightmare, and shouted in his sleep, "God, no!" He bolted from the room, and I found him on the sofa in the living room, hunched over, rocking back and forth slightly, the tee shirt he insisted on wearing to bed against my protests (I wanted as much skin as possible) soaked through. When I touched him, he recoiled and almost took a swing at me. He had a haunted look on his face when he looked up, "Sorry, Nick, so sorry. I just have these episodes. This time it may have been the backfire or Chris dying, I don't really know what sets it off."

"Does it happen often?" I started massaging his back gently.

"Sometimes. Depends."

"So the bit about 'Philina's Song'? About the pleasures of night?"

"More a wish than a guarantee. Anyhow, you saw on the way to the restaurant it can happen when I'm awake too."

"Do you ever go to see somebody about it, I mean a doctor."

"Uh-uh. That sort of thing goes in your record, and it doesn't help. Anyhow, nobody cares about Vietnam vets. Don't you know, we were all criminals."

"I don't think so."

"In a way I do, at least, I think we had no business going there. Look, you go back to bed, and I'll be there in just a little bit." When he did come back to bed, he had stripped down. I was sleeping on my side. He put both arms around me and then started to make love, not very forcefully, but just gentle fondling, which seemed to relieve his tension and sent him off to sleep.

At breakfast I told him I planned to attend Chris's funeral if I could, "His brother will call me about it."

"That'd bring you up near my neck of the woods. Do you still think you'd like to visit West Point?"

"If you're there, do you need to ask?"

He smiled as if the terror from night before had never happened, "I thought so. Just let me know the schedule, and I'll book guest quarters. I can show you around where I was a cadet. We can go out to dinner across the river at a really fancy place on the water ('My treat this time,' I insisted.), and then I might be able to wangle a pass for a weekend in New York."

"But you'll have your teaching," I objected.

"They don't really open the term until July. That's when the entering class checks in and goes through a kind of basic training. So except for orienting myself in my department, I'll have a little more free time than later. I don't have any real duties until classes begin. I hope a visit right away isn't pushing things."

"Actually, I think it'd help me get over the past few weeks. And it'd give me something to look forward to, know what I mean?"

We followed the plan. The next week I flew to Philadelphia, took a train to Villanova, where the Caldwells' extensive properties lay. Rob met me at the station and deposited me at the large guest house on their estate. They scheduled the service for Wednesday morning, and without any explanation, Joan Caldwell had me seated just behind the family. The service was stiffly Episcopalian, and I did everything I could not to reveal the emotional storm inside me. The hardest moments came at the graveside committal in a family burial ground, the ultimate farewell, "All that the Father giveth me shall come to me; and him that cometh to me I will in no wise cast out." But it felt like casting out—or away. We each threw a handful of dirt on Chris's coffin and then went to the house for a reception. When his family introduced me, they gracefully added, "This is one of Chris's professors from Pulpitville." Nobody was so rude as to inquire further. Despite my inner turmoil, I found I could make small talk and related Chris's merits as a student, which stretched the truth only a bit, since I never had him in class. But the pose worked: everybody regarded me as an ambassador graciously provided by the University.

After a much smaller family luncheon, Joan Caldwell in her slightly superior way invited me to a short private audience in her study, "I thank you for coming, Nicholas. Christopher thought so highly of you. I and my family do also. Will we ever see you again?"

"I would guess not. This has been painful."

She seemed to understand, her aloof composure never betraying the slightest fracture, "Don't blame yourself for what happened. He wasn't your responsibility in the end, or mine, or anybody's. It's comforting to me, though, that he knew even for a little while that very special kind of . . ." she searched for a neutral word, "companionship with another human being. You made his life better, if not longer. You will always enjoy my family's gratitude for that. Farewell," the audience concluded. And I had the distinct impression that she considered an inconvenient episode in her son's life now closed forever.

As I rode the train from Philadelphia to New York, I stared at my reflection in the plate glass, hoping that the other passengers wouldn't notice when my eyes welled up and an isolated tear or two ran down my cheek. The iron wheels seemed to chant:

> Fear no more the lightning-flash,
>   Nor th'all-dreaded thunderstone;
> Fear not slander, censure rash;
>   Thou hast finished joy and moan:
> All lovers young, all lovers must
> Consign to thee, and come to dust.
>
> No exorciser harm thee!
>   Nor no witchcraft charm thee!
> Ghost unlaid forbear thee!
>   Nothing ill come near thee!
> Quiet consummation have;
> And renowned be thy grave!

But I could never banish Chris's ghost entirely. The people we truly love haunt our thoughts unremittingly for the rest of our lives, a little more intensely with each passing year, the grief slowly evanescing like lost wax to leave only the enduringly sculpted affection beneath.

15 MIGRATION

When I stepped off the train at a stop on the Hudson north of New York, Scott met me with a determined look, prepared for the worst. In those days gay men didn't indulge even the slightest "public display of affection"—banned for all soldiers in uniform at any event. So I shook hands as warmly as decorum allowed and threw my luggage in the trunk. After we both climbed in, he asked, "How are you holding up?"

"Doing all right. If you had asked me earlier, when I started from Phili, I might have said differently. But I've had some time to sort things out. Just drained now," I paused, then added, "You know the hardest thing?"

"No, what?" He meant to let me talk it out.

"The finality of throwing a handful of dirt onto a casket. The very tangible confirmation that you'll never see somebody you lived with, and slept with, made love to, attended church with, never see him smile again or hear his voice."

"I understand. If a buddy dies in combat, they ship the body home, and we say final goodbyes in a memorial ceremony. It never seems right, either way."

"I need to move on."

"Best course. Look, if you're up for it, the on-post club has a bar that stays open 'til 11. So we could catch a drink and a bite to eat. Just pub food."

"Sounds great, I'm starved. I lived through a reception and a meager family luncheon in Villanova."

"Tough going with the family?"

"No. They treated me, well, like a figure from their son's past they hoped not to see again. But I shouldn't complain: at least they included me."

"That's something." He wisely shifted focus, "Let's look forward to your stay here."

"I might be able to do that," I flashed him smile. "Just one more thing, major Major."

"And the sarcasm begins," he objected. "I think I liked 'drained' better. Have fun while you can, because I'm on the list for promotion to Lieutenant Colonel."

"Really? Sure it's not a mistake? Colonel Colonel doesn't have the same ring. It sounds like a fried-chicken franchise."

"Didn't I offer to break your face once before?"

"I remember taking a pass then, and I'll take a pass now."

"Okay, then no more lip, Herr Doktor Professor."

I groaned, "I deserved that, but here's my question anyhow: how has your bogus reason for my visit here played?"

He sighed with the long-suffering patience accorded a small child, "They didn't teach you anything about subtle misdirection for your Ph.D., did they? It's totally plausible: you're a faculty colleague in my field of German studies, and I met you at a library in West Berlin."

"Met me in a library? That's what you call that place? The one with nothing but randy men inside, all drinking? You and I were doing serious research, and you followed me to my apartment for consultation."

"That was low. I distinctly remember you inviting me home, or at least offering only token resistance.

Anyhow, wait until you see the club. It's on testosterone overload too, and *all* of the guys are military."

"I enjoy clubs on base thoroughly!"

"I bet. Is there anybody in the services, any guy in fatigues or a uniform who doesn't turn you on?"

I paused a long time for dramatic effect, "I'm trying to think. I prefer Army men for the most part"—I tried to get a rise—"but marines, sailors, Coast Guard, firemen, policemen, they all sizzle, even when they're in civies, like you the first time we met."

"Any more on the list?"

"Not that occur to me at the moment, but I'll think about that one."

"Let me give you some really good advice: you better start 'preferring' Army guys a whole lot, not just 'for the most part,' because you're surround by about 5000 plus, any of whom will rip your throat out if you so much as mention marines or sailors. Oh, and not to spoil your fantasy, but they admit women too."

"I dated women a long time ago. But now my motto runs: so many men, so little time," I offered, egging him on. "If I take them in large groups . . . ," I mused idly.

"You better just take one."

"Promise?"

"You're totally depraved. Anyhow, on post we're not going to have a chance, got that straight?"

"I didn't think you could get anything straight."

"Headline: 'College Professor Meets Unfortunate Demise in Mysterious Fall from Hudson River Bluff.'"

"Which is just what you're doing now, bluffing. I wish we could kiss."

"I have a reputation to keep up around here."

"I bet."

"Okay, that's enough out of you. We check you into your room and then go marinate some ice cubes. I think I remember Johnny Walker Black."

"It's the family name, after all. And maybe in my room I can get just *one* kiss?"

"No deal. You're on report for general misbehavior, and I'm not even helping you up to your quarters. We'd get carried away and blow our cover."

"Hmmm, an interesting choice of words." He briefly shook his head in despair, waited downstairs while I left my bags, and then conducted me through the soft night air to the West Point Club.

Because Scott didn't know many people at the Academy yet, the other men at the bar mostly left us alone. When one of his fellow department members walked up, he introduced me as a professor of German history from Pulpitville, which gained me some respect. We each had a burger and a couple of rounds of drinks, and perhaps I had another round or two to help smooth the end of a strenuous day.

When we returned, somewhat intoxicated, to the guest quarters I was assigned, I begged Scott to come up to my room to say goodnight. Once we were inside, I couldn't keep from initiating a private but nevertheless strictly prohibited display of affection, which took the form of prolonged kissing. He cautioned, "Take it easy, Nick, the walls are thin here."

"Then you'll need to be super quiet," and before he could stop me, I unzipped him.

"Don't, Nick!" he whispered.

"You can always shout for help." He didn't seem so inclined.

After he finished, I commented, "See, that wasn't so hard. Correction: 'so difficult.'"

He looked down and smiled, "You think you're so cute, don't you? I have half a notion to leave you there." But he helped me up, unzipped me, and then warned again, "Be quiet," as he returned the favor.

When we were done, I looked him square in the eye, "You planned this, didn't you, because you knew I'd be frustrated and willing."

He flashed me one of those complicit grins that sometimes appears after sex, "I'm not admitting to anything. But that's all you get 'til New York. Now I gotta go. I'll come round about 9:30, after I've worked out. And then I'll show you the place."

During the Revolutionary War the Army chose the site of West Point for its command of the Hudson River and only later converted it from a fort to a military academy. We toured the grounds, visited the cemetery, had lunch at the club, which in the daylight offered a spectacular view of the valley below. For West Point offered not only a venerable tradition but also inspiring scenic grandeur. The striking landscape rekindled my recently depressed sense of adventure:

> He whom God would show His favor,
> Is sent into the wider world,
> To taste His wonders' glorious savor
> In hill, wood, stream, and field unfurl'd.
>
> The lazy who stay homebound lying,
> Ne'er behold the dawning's red,
> They only know of children's crying,
> Care and labor, need for bread.

The riv'lets from the mountains springing,
The larks who soar so high with joy,
Shall I not join them in my singing
With fullest voice in glad alloy?

I leave the good Lord sole command;
With riv'let, lark and hill and field,
With earth and heaven in His hand,
He knows for me what they best yield.

As we continued our stroll through campus after lunch, various cadets and lower-ranking soldiers saluted Scott. And I must have betrayed my awe, for he finally asked in a very low voice, "Look, is it the fact that they salute me, or that you're proud to be seen in the company of a handsome major?"

"Who's that?" I teased. "Must I choose one of those? This doesn't impress you anymore?"

"It still impresses me."

"And the handsome college professor?"

"Even more so. On that note, let's get a move on. We'll go over to a posh little restaurant I know across the river, and it's a drive."

"What should I wear?"

"Coat and tie. I'll go civilian too. It's supposed to be a place for romantic dates."

"You should find one, in that case."

"Very funny. Do you remember last night?"

"That wasn't romantic, that was electric!"

"I thought it was both. But no more of that here."

"Everything's prohibited?" I pouted.

"Not letting you off your leash again until tomorrow in New York. Then whatever you want."

"You're braver than I thought. I've been looking forward to this for a week. I'm a very frustrated and unfulfilled man."

He smirked, "That's the idea. And I think I'm pretty brave."

We set out for New York at mid-morning the next day. That magnificent edifice to human industry held more wonders. We arrived on Friday afternoon, had dinner and some recreation that night (He felt as frustrated and deprived as I).

Then on Saturday, Scott surprised me just when I thought I had him figured out, "I have tickets to Lincoln Center tonight."

"Really? What's on? Opera?" I guessed because I had taken him to the Staatsoper in Berlin.

"Opera season's over. *Swan Lake*, ballet," he answered, obviously proud of himself.

"You did this to impress me?"

"I bought the tickets in order to have a nice evening and because I really like classical dance."

Now you may not believe that I tried hard to suppress a grin, but I did. I inclined my head downward a bit and put a finger over my lips. It didn't work.

"What's so funny?" he asked, a little irritated.

"Well, don't misunderstand me: I like ballet too, Tchaikovsky in particular. I just wouldn't have pegged your for a balletomane."

"A what?"

"A ballet fan. A tough West Point-trained major, soon-to-be lieutenant colonel. It's just . . . " I started to chuckle softly.

"Just what?"

"Men in tights? Do I need to explain?"

"Very handsome muscular men in tights lifting their partners over their heads. Try it some time, you cultural cretin."

"Don't get personal—I dated a classical dancer once."

He rolled his eyes, "I'm beginning to believe you dated everybody once." He added a bit defensively, "*Swan Lake* has a touching story: impossible love leading to doom. Perhaps yours tonight."

"You're a romantic and *so* gay."

"You'd better hope so later on."

"I'd love to see the ballet. But about tonight: I don't think I can pick you up off the floor, let alone lift you overhead."

"And here I thought you were a real man. I myself spend all my other weekends lifting weights, drinking beer, and watching football and baseball."

"I can't imagine why. So it's true, then: they made the uniforms tighter." Even he had to laugh at that. We kidded each other a little more, but we had a wonderful time seeing the newly arrived Vladimir Malakhov dance Prince Siegfried with the American Ballet Theatre. Carried away by the spirit of celebration, Scott suggested we go to a gay bar.

"It's certainly where you belong," I offered, "But are you sure that's going to be all right?"

"Yeah. If we find somewhere discreet, how many West Point men will we see?"

"Discreet," I mused. "I know a place over in the mid 70s off of Lexington. You'd have to hunt to find the entrance. Very upscale, very quiet, mostly older gentlemen in coat and tie, and then some very well-dressed young hustlers."

"Which are you?"

"Funny. I must be the hustler, because you're the older gentleman."

"Okay, enough out of you. You're apparently overlooking the occasionally strand of gray invading those gorgeous brown curls of yours. But lead on."

The joke was on us, because in addition to the quite suave older men and the well-groomed hustlers, we found four young men, obviously military in civies, huddled together. And the moment Scott saw them, he whispered, "Holy Shit! Let's leave!"

"Why, what's the problem?"

"You wouldn't remember him, but over in that corner is a cadet who saw you with me on post, and I mean not from a distance, but while we were walking around. He saluted me when we passed by."

"You're here, I'm here, he's here. We're all 'off limits.'"

"I'd be willing to bet that the other three guys are cadets too. Man, if this gets back to the dean . . . "

"Well, it's a little late, because he's already spotted me, and even though you think he can't see you with your back to him, guess what? Look, you've never dealt with this, at least not as a professor. But I have—often. I can tell you right now, they're a lot more nervous than you, they're wondering what's going to happen, and the worst thing you can do is retreat, especially because they're not the enemy. You need to show them how it works, acknowledge the elephant in the room, so to speak. It'll follow you to West Point tomorrow. Will you let me serve as emissary under a flag of truce?"

"I guess," he allowed reluctantly.

I walked over to the group, all of whom prepared to run for the nearest exit. Not an option, since I stood between them and the entrance, "Gentlemen, do I know any of you?"

A long, embarrassed pause ensued, and then one of them finally looked me straight in the eye and said, "Sir, yes sir. I'm first-year Cadet Rick Turner, sir."

"Rick, I'm Nicholas Walker, a professor of German history at Pulpitville visiting Major Willemer, and you may have noticed me on base. (One of the group muttered, not quietly enough, "We sure did," which garnered a warning glance from Turner.) Now I could lie and say that we came here because we didn't know what kind of place it was. And you could lie and tell me that you're here just looking for a watering hole in the neighborhood and happened on this one. But you'd need to search pretty hard even to find the entrance to this bar. And anyhow, I would guess that deception wouldn't square with your honor code, and it certainly doesn't with mine. So let's put our cards on the table and see how the play."

"Yes sir." By now they all wore an expression of surprise.

"Then it works this way: you start by shaking my hand and introducing your friends."

Rick reached out and even managed to appear less concerned, "You know my name, this is my roommate Jim Archer, that's Steve Lester and his roommate Mark Adams, all rising firsties."

"Which I'm guessing means 'rising seniors'?"

"Yes sir."

"Do you want to meet Major Willemer? Because you'll see him at on campus." I motioned for Scott to join us, which he did with composure, though I could see him sweat just a bit. They all came unobtrusively to attention at his approach, until he commanded softly, "At ease, gentlemen." As I introduced him, the young men addressed him as "Major."

After the introductions, the cadets overcame their initial embarrassment, and youthful curiosity took over, "Could we ask the Major whether that's a West Point class ring?" one of them ventured.

"Class of 1970. You men ordered yours?"

"Yes sir," they answered quietly but emphatically.

"Congrats, gentlemen. Let's go sit in the corner over there and talk. Assuming that none of us will cross paths in class, which would create a situation, I want you to tell me about yourselves."

This invitation elicited a barrage of information. Rick pretty clearly served as spokesman, "So we're all gay (spoken so earnestly and anxiously, that I resisted throwing in a sarcastic, 'You don't say.'). We've been sharing quarters for the past two years, I mean, Jim with me, Steve with Adam."

Scott took over, "Just roommates? Permission to speak freely."

A couple of them colored visibly, but Rick continued for the group, "We're pretty committed to our respective, ah, buddies."

"Sweet deal," I offered.

At this point Mark couldn't contain himself, "It's great! I mean, while we keep it under wraps, we have a little time to, well, 'be together.'" ("Not as much was we'd like," Steve added aside.)

Rick shot another look of admonition, but Scott reassured, "I'm sure you guys stick by one another"

Rick stepped in with a nonstop stream, "We plan to go on being 'partners' after we graduate—haven't figured that one out. And, Major, were you, I mean did you have any experience when you were a cadet; did you know you were gay; what about Professor Walker, I mean how long have you known him and . . . ?"

Scott interrupted him with, "Slow down, Mr. Turner. As for my four years at West Point, no I didn't know then I was gay. Only after I reached Vietnam. You'll need to ask Dr. Walker, I mean Nick, about where we met, since he has a lot more 'experience' than I," he glanced sideways at me to see if this elicited a reaction, which it did.

"Gentlemen, Major Willemer and I met in Berlin about four months ago. He was sitting in a bar by himself, lonesome and crying in his beer—completely understandable, considering he's homely and not very funny. And I unfortunately happened to sit down beside him. And he must not have that much 'experience,' because he started reciting poetry. And when that bizarre tactic failed, he used the most tired pickup line in the book, 'Can I buy you a drink?'"

"Works on you every time," Scott offered.

"Who's telling this story?" I objected. "Continuing on, he then claimed he couldn't make it back to base in his pathetic condition. So out of the kindness of my heart, I offered to let him sleep on the sofa in my apartment, where he then tried to take advantage of me."

"Successfully. In fact, you encouraged me," Scott countered.

"You had me liquored up, Major," I replied to Scott, then turned back to the group, "He somehow managed to wheedle his way into my bedroom, and the rest is," I gave a resigned sigh, "history. We dated for the next couple of months, and we're seeing whether we'd like to continue our relationship."

"You're so easy," Scott interjected.

"But gentlemen," I continued, "He's getting demerits for bad behavior, and as a result he's sleeping on the sofa tonight."

"Our room doesn't have a sofa," Scott observed.

"My point exactly. You'll book a separate room . . . in a different hotel, just to prove that I'm not as 'easy' as you've suggested to these upstanding young men."

By this time the cadets were convulsed from trying to stifle their laughter. Mark inserted another question to break up the routine, "How have you kept this under wraps, sir? Steve and I, really all of us have a hard time flying under the radar."

"It's tough, as you can plainly see, since Nick's impossible," Scott gave me a not-so-gentle pat on the shoulder. "I try to keep him in line, and I wish I didn't need to. But what can I say, he worships me."

"A hotel in Brooklyn," I countered, "I'm leaving with these men." (And you out there: no, I didn't imagine a five-way with four cadets—okay, maybe for a second as a remote fantasy.)

"Why didn't I see that coming? You're incorrigible." But Scott then became serious, "I won't lie to you guys: it bothers me a lot that we can't date except in secret or even show open affection except in places like this. The stealth takes a toll."

At this Rick jumped in assertively, "Sir, to be frank, we're part of a group. I don't just mean us, but graduates going back for a long time. We don't exactly have an organization yet. But we have an informal network. And some of the guys are advocating for gay men to serve openly and even get married some day."

"Do you honestly think any of that is remotely possible? Homosexuals in the Army, getting married? Sounds like a stretch to me," I expressed doubtfully.

Scott's solidarity asserted itself in his students' defense, "Army men can be pretty determined, Nick. If they set their mind on an objective, they'll fight for it until they win. Don't underestimate them." Then he turned back to the cadets, "Gentlemen, all this is confidential, of course. But if you ever need advice or help, come around to talk with me."

"Appreciate that, sir," Rick answered, "Oh, and by the way, Professor Walker, just for the record, we think you should, well, cut the Major some slack. I mean, give him the benefit of your 'experience' tonight." The cadets cracked up.

"Army guys look out for each other, Nick," Scott tried unsuccessfully to suppress his amusement.

"Just when I started to like this bunch," I replied with mock aggravation. "I'll take it under consideration, but 'the Major' shouldn't get his hopes up, considering tonight's bad conduct." And after we shot the breeze for another hour and finished our drinks, we left the bar to go our separate ways.

"See," I offered to Scott as we strolled back to our hotel, "That turned out fine."

"We'll find out."

"Is it so unusual for you to be in the same bar as some of your troops?"

"During the war, no, to a certain point. The enlisted men, sergeants, lieutenants, all the men in a platoon or a company would drink together. But always aware of rank. The unit needed to relax after the grim things we saw on patrol. On the other hand, captains and above kept to themselves."

"Do you really think gay men will serve openly in the military or that we'll be allowed to marry?"

"They're young and idealistic. What could it hurt if they tried to work for a better life."

"Hurt? I think it's going to hurt a lot—backlash from the bigots who preach hate openly and oppose freedom of sexual orientation violently. And covert resistance from a lot of so-called liberals who support gay rights publically but loathe it in their secret heart of hearts. I live in a town full of 'open-minded' people who just plain don't like the idea of men having sex with one another. And on that note, tell me honestly: you had no inkling as cadet?"

"No," he hesitated—he clearly didn't want to discuss much about his first gay experiences. He knew a good deal of my exploits, but all I could pull out of him was, "It started in Hawaii when I was on R 'n' R. It's not worth talking about."

"See—even you're uncomfortable discussing it." But Scott just lapsed into an evasive silence.

Our night back at the hotel began romantically. But after he fell asleep, Scott had another nightmare and started screaming. I switched on the light, and he awoke with a start, looked around, realized where he was, and then turned away from me.

"What triggered it?" I tried to coax.

"Maybe encountering the cadets, anxiety over whether they'll really keep it to themselves or whether they can. But I know I can't do this my whole life, lead a covert existence." Scott wouldn't recount the nightmare at all. He walled a part of himself off and clearly didn't want to talk about his earlier experiences. It takes a lifetime to know somebody thoroughly; even then, some compartments remain too painfully locked to open.

When we awakened in the late morning, Scott invited me to lunch before my flight left. I thought it a good omen that he was reluctant to have me go, and I wondered whether I would finally receive an explanation for the episodes of anxiety he seemed to be experiencing with increasing regularity (the diagnosis of post-traumatic stress disorder had just recently appeared, but it didn't have wide currency among the general public, and Scott still refused to see a doctor about what he regarded simply as bad dreams).

At lunch he had two important questions to ask, "So, now that we've spent a little bit of time after Berlin, what do you think? Do you want to continue, seeing me, I mean?" The hopeful and plaintive tone of Scott's voice demanded an unequivocal answer.

"Definitely," I offered without pause.

"Great, because I have a plan. I've introduced you around as an expert in German history. What if I somehow arranged a visiting professorship at West Point for a year on the basis of your position at Pulpitville?"

He was a little put off by my equivocal response, "If I don't remain Pulpitville, the University couldn't agree to an academic exchange: I may apply for jobs someplace else this summer."

"Where? As a professor? The academic year's almost started. Anyhow, you just gained tenure."

"I don't care, I'm going to look. I have no idea where—I simply know I can't stay much longer."

"Because of Chris?"

"That's a part of it, but just a small part. Bad memories of dealing with some colleagues—the hateful morons who tried to deny me tenure. They're not going to forgive or forget that I fought against dismissal successfully. Then there's the whole Southern charade, the general dislike of 'foreigners,' and all the empty pretentiousness. I'm suffocating in that town."

Scott revealed a little disquiet about this reply, "It's your life, Nick. Just realize, I'm assigned for three years to teach at West Point. That's firm. Then I only have a year to go, and maybe I'll look for a posting somewhere else. Remember, there are Army bases near Pulpitville if you stay. I'm sure I can find something for that last bit of time. We'd both be free to live wherever we wanted after that."

I remained noncommittal. "I appreciate the sentiment behind that thought, truly I do. Nothing would please me more than to spend more time together. But it might be risky for you, so let's think it over and see how it plays out."

Making it clear he wouldn't abandon a plan he had formed in his mind, he simply replied somewhat reservedly, "Okay. We can decide when we get there," which closed off further discussion.

We parted at Grand Central, he on a train up the Hudson, I on a subway to the airport, summoning the distant recollection of a similar scene in that exact setting so many years ago. He risked a hug, and I left him with regret, as I always seemed to be doing with men I held in affection.

When I returned to Pulpitville, I immediately began to cast around for open positions in academic trade journals. The most promising and immediate job was one in Washington with a consulting firm that specialized in organizing applications to the National Endowment for the Humanities and the National Endowment for the Arts for outside clients—universities with major projects, even documentary film production companies. The firm had an opening for a grant writer at quite a good salary, and I sent off a resume with all the items requested, thinking nothing much would come of it. Just after the application deadline I received a phone call from the head of human resources, asking if I could come for an interview in a week. *Why not*, I thought, *nothing to lose*, and I travelled to D.C. for a day without telling anybody.

When I arrived at the firm's offices in Georgetown, I spoke with the executives about a job shepherding proposals for scholarly editions and translation projects. The attraction lay in the ability to shape the course of research by American scholars and in the colleagues with whom I would work (a welcoming and informed crew). The spacious private offices marked a step up from the institutional drabness of the University. The drawbacks lay in the lack of job security (my projects had to sustain me by bringing in fees) and in the workload. It would be quite a change from the life of a college professor who met his classes several hours a week each semester, with three months of summer break when I could work at my own pace.

About two weeks later, in the middle of July, they offered me the position. In addition to much better pay, I saw clear advantages to D.C. over Pulpitville. I was like an animal gnawing off a foot to escape the trap of the Southern Mystique in a stifling backwater posing as a cultural center. In Washington I would enjoy cosmopolitan surroundings and the ability to see Scott in the time it took the Metroliner to go from Union Station to Penn Station. I took the position with less than a month to move.

You would have thought that I had walked naked across the quads to hear the reaction of my department chair, "This is outrageous! You owe us timely notice, and you're obligated to teach all of next year."

"There's absolutely no clause in my contract or my research grant requiring me to teach another year," I objected. "So what 'obligates' me?"

"The simple good manners of a gentleman," he drawled, repeating the outworn chivalric code that administrators used to subjugate faculty in that Southern fantasy land. "Nobody leaves the University six weeks before the beginning of the fall semester."

"I'm going to. After the attempt to deny me tenure, I owe you nothing." End of discussion. I wanted to add that if Dean Barnard (The Stripper) had any objections, *he* could walk naked across the quads to raise them.

Elated, I called Scott, "Great news: I've resigned from Tennelina and taken a job with a consulting firm in D.C. I start in three weeks." I heard nothing on the line, "Scott?"

"So let me get this straight, Nick. You're giving up permanent tenure the year after you fought for it? To take a job with no guarantee they won't fire you on two weeks' notice, and you want me to congratulate you? Just when I spent the last month persuading the head of the history department here to invite you for a whole year as a visiting professor. And you were going to warn me about this in advance?"

"I told you I was considering a change, Major."

"Colonel now, and I deserved the details."

"Excuse me, Colonel, sir. I am informing you now, sir. I just didn't think it required prior clearance from the Army, sir. Besides, there's a substantial upgrade in my pay, sir."

He groaned when I quoted the figure, "That's more than I make."

"Well, for one thing, I'll be living in a much more expensive city, though a much nicer and far more interesting one."

"So you can cruise the bars there?"

"From somebody surrounded by thousands of randy young men that's completely unfair," I protested. "You're just at 'the Academy' so you can cruise the cadets?" Silence. "I haven't looked at anybody else since Berlin. And by the way, my salary recognizes seven years of graduate school, three foreign languages, a Ph.D., the dissertation, and two books. They call that expertise and experience."

"Oh, I know about your 'experience.' And Ph.D. must stand for 'phony dickhead.'"

I couldn't let that pass, "You picked a great time to become clever. But look at it this way: it's a straight shot up to New York, and I can meet you there on a moment's notice when you can get a weekend pass."

"I wouldn't have needed a pass if you had lived here next year," he replied in an injured and disappointed tone.

"Now let's see," I became truly angry, "How would that work? Oh, I understand now: lunch every day at 'the Club,' romantic dinners across the Hudson, trips to New York to watch ballet and visit the gay bars. Receptions and cocktail parties we attend together on post as what, 'just friends'? Nobody will notice that we spend all our time with each other and think that, well, maybe we're doing it in your quarters or in mine. You must have drunk the same Kool-Aid up there as your crusading cadets.

"Then there's crossing campus holding hands, working out mornings together and having sex in the showers afterwards for the amusement of the other officers. And then comes your court-martial, dishonorable discharge for conduct unbecoming and sodomy, not to mention loss of my visiting professorship and then my tenured job at the most homophobic 'liberal' university accredited in the U.S. God, you're so brilliant, Colonel. Except you think more with your cock than your brains."

"Oh, it's so good to learn that you don't always talk like you have a stick up your ass!"

"Unless it's your stick!"

"Apparently that's all I thought about when I hooked up with you in Berlin," came the heated retort.

Ouch! I slammed the receiver down, ran the argument over in my mind for about thirty seconds, and picked the phone up to redial. His line was busy. Who would he call? His CO, his department chair, his mother? I tried again, still busy. So I gave up.

The moment I hung up the phone the second time, it rang. "Nick?" it was Scott, "You there?"

"Yes," I said, dejected and ashamed.

We both started to apologize at once, until he insisted, "Just listen. I don't know what got into me. I miss you so much. I still had this crazy plan for us to live together somehow. Totally unrealistic, but the thought of three years long distance just seems unbearable. It aches how much I miss you after only a month."

"No, look, it's my fault. I should've told you about the application. But I couldn't be sure what would happen, so it was pointless beforehand. And I'm trying to get closer, if only by a couple of hours. It stinks, but we're just going to have to live with it for a while. If I hadn't met you after Chris, I'd be the loneliest man in the world. I . . . "

"No, I'd be the loneliest," he corrected, "I've been the loneliest. I was beginning to fall apart when I met you, and as crazy as I am, you're what keeps from going totally over the edge. You don't know how much I love you." It had always been implied in our conversations, but never uttered.

I had to make good on that declaration fast, "If I didn't love you, we wouldn't just have had our first fight. I can't see whether you're smiling. A little bit?"

"A lot. And congrats on the job. You deserve to be happy. And you deserve the pay too. I was just jealous."

"I can write a letter to the Superintendent. My boyfriend is sexy and smart: he needs a raise. Think it'll work?" Silence "I don't think so either, but there ought to be a regulation somewhere."

"You'd make a great military spouse."

"I don't think so. I don't play politics well."

"Not on the surface, maybe. But deep down you've won me over entirely. . . . I wish I could come down there to help you move, but it's a no-go."

"Oh, I think I can get up a detail to manage. You just need to stay in touch, as often as you can. Because I long for the sound of your voice every minute of every day."

"Well, I know my objective now: to find a posting near you after I finish my tour here. Until then, I'm going to call a lot, just to make sure you aren't misbehaving—too much. 'Duty, Honor . . .'"

"Colonel, ah, I mean 'Country.'"

The move to D.C. was hectic but gratifying. I said a prayer as I departed the Pulpitville town limits, vowing never again to revisit that benighted fantasy land. I found a small apartment in Northwest, not too far from Dupont Circle, and I began to enjoy my new job with some very amiable colleagues. Scott's three-year appointment seemed to last an eternity, but we met in New York when he could arrange a pass. He came down for Thanksgiving but still spent his Christmas leaves in Nebraska, stopping to celebrate New Year's Eve with me in Washington. I wondered what his last year of service would look like and where the Army would post him. I expected we would be separated, and I didn't look forward to being apart for yet another year. The only silver lining seemed to be that, as we spent more time together, however brief, Scott appeared to calm down a bit, his nightmares receding.

16 *PLAUDITE AMICI*

Toward the end of Scott's stint at West Point he called me, beginning as usual with innocuously jocular pleasantries, "How's it going down there among our nation's movers and shakers cruising Dupont Circle?"

"Tricked out. And for you at the end of your final term on your five-thousand-man military stud farm?"

"Exhausted from all those communal showers, so they're giving me time off before my next posting."

"Great! Come down and shower with *me*."

"Might do that."

His terse and somewhat cryptic answers signaled something up his sleeve, and I had to play along, "Good. And where are they sending you next?"

"Oh, this administrative job. Aide to some general or other."

"Congratulations! So how much time before you need to report."

"Not much. Maybe a week. I've tried hard to wangle a really cushy assignment. I wanted Hawaii—on the beach among scantily clad men. Instead, they decided to send me to Washington," he dropped nonchalantly.

His coyness demanded revenge, so I concealed my elation—with some difficulty—"Seattle's a long flight, climate's cold and rainy. I'll miss seeing you."

"Listen, you jerk . . ."

"It's your own fault for stringing me on, Colonel."

"No excuses, sir. D.C., sir. This large office building filled with bureaucrats—tedious: the Pentagon."

"You'll need to find someplace to live."

"With you."

"Totally impractical; small apartment." I objected.

"Then we'll need to get a house, won't we?"

I could no longer suppress a yelp of delight, followed by "You could've told me right away and you're lucky you're not standing here, because I'd kill you."

"Threats of domestic violence so soon?" he quipped, "Before I even move in?"

"Moving in remains to be seen. Retirement?"

"I won't file my paperwork until right at the end. And believe me, when the Super told me about Washington, I could have kissed him."

"I suspected as much: trading sexual favors for influence. And here I thought . . . ," I fell silent.

"Just kidding; you're cuter." More silence. "Okay, you're a lot cuter, in fact, you're the most handsome guy I've ever seen and the only one I kiss. Satisfied?"

"Don't stop."

"That's what you usually say. Now listen up, they'll give me a generous allowance 'cause it's D.C. And I've saved a pretty fair amount. Maybe you've saved a little too (I had), and we can buy a place together. We'll put both our names on the deed. I'm thinking a modest house in Arlington."

"That's a wonderful thought. But will it raise any suspicion because you're living with a man?"

"They taught you nothing about tactical misdirection in your years of education. Of course I'll be living with a guy; they call it 'sharing quarters.' Happens all the time in D.C. Washington's an expensive place to live. They don't need to know we own jointly. I'll just tell everybody we share rent or I rent from you."

"Oh, now you're a kept man. I like that: I give the orders. When do we start looking?"

"You're totally out of control as usual. I'll stay with you while we look at real estate."

"Only if you're on good behavior."

"My best!" He knew exactly what I had in mind: destroying a mattress and house hunting.

"Can we put a sex-slave clause in the mortgage?"

"Very funny. I'm trying to be serious."

"So am I. Do I have any say in this?" Silence on the end of the line. "Yes sir, Colonel, sir!" We found a bungalow that we could afford on a quiet street in Arlington, moved in, and set up house.

Now you'll remember my appalling domestic relationships from the past, and true to form, living with Scott began with a dramatic explosion (an omen of things to come, as it turned out). He decided to surprise me with breakfast on our first morning together, and he concluded it didn't take a rocket scientist to light our old range to broil sausage. In fact, Scott did learn about the basic physics of expanding gases—the hard way. He turned on the oven, then walked to the other side of the room to retrieve a match. A dull thud in the kitchen—the accumulated gas in the oven igniting—followed by a rich string of profanities jolted me out of bed. I rushed into the kitchen, "Are you burned?"

"I'm mostly okay, but I singed my eyebrows off," he admitted ruefully.

"You light the match first, *then* you turn on the gas, poor bulldog. You're lucky you didn't blow the whole house up." I started laughing uncontrollably, "There's always eyebrow pencil." He winced.

I discovered he was altogether helpless in the kitchen, "Have you ever done *any* cooking?"

"You're kidding, right? I went immediately from my parents' home into the Army and never had to cook anything in my life. I can open a can of rations, uh, sort of."

I shook my head, "How about coffee in the morning?"

"I wouldn't count on it. I once burned spaghetti."

"That's not possible."

"It is if you let the water boil away."

The "notorious oven detonation" occasioned a set of kitchen rules posted on the refrigerator door:

1. Any kitchen appliance capable of heating food—including the microwave—is off limits to officers of the U.S. Army (he grimaced).

2. No drinking out of the milk carton or the orange-juice bottle (he pouted a bit).

3. U.S. Army officers may make a bowl of cereal but must place their dishes in the dishwasher.

4. Infractions are punishable by exile to the sofa for not less than one nor more than seven nights. (He objected, "Cruel and unusual punishment is banned under the Geneva Convention.")

Scott took what he termed my "domestic tyranny" in good humor, however, accustomed as he was to the order created by decades of military discipline, not to mention his appreciation for my culinary skills. And the Army had trained him to be fairly neat, he didn't mind housekeeping, and he could handle odd repairs with the best of them (he had picked this up as a boy on the ranch). After almost a year of having a really good time living together, flying very discretely under the radar at various gay bars in D.C., going to the movies, to the theater, to concerts, to restaurants, he filed his retirement papers.

"What are you going to do after you retire?" I asked idly one afternoon as he returned from one of his last days at his Pentagon office.

"I'll receive a pension, but I'm only 42—I need to keep working. I have a line on a position with a lobbying firm."

"Joining the K-Street mafia? Will they care that you're living in sin with a man? I mean, at 42 it's not too hard to figure out."

"Ah, I didn't tell you the result of meeting those cadets our first time in New York."

"I knew you were getting it on with the troops up there while I was suffering here in celibate denial. And you call me 'experienced,'" I teased.

"Nothing like that. You have an impossibly dirty mind."

"You like that," I pointed out.

"Technicality."

"Try that tonight, my friend."

But he was not to be diverted from his tale of triumph, "Anyhow, Mark Adams and Steve Lester made an appointment with me in my office at the beginning of their last semester. They were glum."

"I've seen that with students. Parting depression: they don't know what's going to come next."

Plaudite Amici

"Well in the Army they knew exactly what would come next: a minimum of five years' service in return for their free ride at the Academy and then some time in the active reserve. And that meant going wherever their posting took them, almost certainly not together or even close to each other. Mark said that they didn't think they could face the separation, that they were thinking of dropping out."

"In their last semester?"

"Exactly. A crazy idea, but they were pretty low."

"What did you tell them?"

"First, I reminded them that the Army would require them to repay their tuition if they didn't finish and serve their five years, and the bill would be substantial. Second, changing posts every three years is a standard feature of military life. Even if they were straight and married or engaged, they would need to endure long separations—part of the job and what they signed up for when they enrolled in West Point. They were lucky to share quarters at the Academy (and I didn't ask how they had managed that one), but now the time to sacrifice for the sake of duty had arrived. And then, I hope you'll forgive me, I used our situation as an illustration, how we kept in touch, how we met when we could but not often enough."

"Thank God it's behind us now. But what has that to do with a lobbying position?"

"The cadets thanked me for the advice. I don't think they'll last beyond their five-year obligation, but they did volunteer the names of some former West Point grads 'in the network.' And that's how I made contact with the K-street group. They're lobbying the administration and Congress for HIV research, gay marriage, and open service in the armed forces. So you can imagine that almost all the members of the firm are gay or lesbian ex-military. I've met them, and they bring their partners to office parties. We're going to have a lot more freedom, the kind of freedom I've always wanted to live my life publicly and not incidentally to show off my partner. And I mean to tell my parents about us."

"Compliment noted as well as your courageous support of lost causes. Do you think this will play well with your folks? It's different for me. My parents already know pretty much what's going on, because I came out to them. And anybody I live with must be 'involved.' I've only avoided telling them what you did for a living because I didn't want to hurt your career. But your parents don't have a clue about any of it."

"Their problem. In the meantime," all of a sudden Scott became very nervous, something atypical, and he started rummaging around in his briefcase, "Damn, where is it?"

"What?"

Completely flustered now, he located the item he wanted, and then he turned to me and stuttered out, "Uh, just to make it official, uh, formal—oh Christ, I picked this up for you on the way home . . ." Words wouldn't carry him any further, and so he simply held out a small jewel box. I opened it to find a simple, elegant man's gold ring with a black star sapphire, surrounded on either side by two very small inset diamond chips, glinting in the afternoon sun.

"I suppose you want me to wear it?"

"On your left hand," his face flushed deeply, "Army colors. If you need time to think it over . . ."

He would never get it all out, so I interrupted, "I don't need time to 'think it over.' The answer is 'yes,' to the wish in your mind and the one in your heart." By this time he had gone scarlet from hyperventilating and seemed ready to collapse. "Of course, we can't spend the rest of our lives together if you die right now of asphyxiation. Permission to breathe free-ly, Colonel. And after you start doing that, don't say anything more, just kiss me."

"Every time I kiss you, I think I'm going to stop breathing."

"Let's risk it."

> From yonder village comes a lad,
> To walk his lover home.
> He leads him past the willow sad,
> And lets his musings roam:
>
> "Now if you suffer grief and shame
> Because you honor me,
> Our love will end yet all the same
> As quick as flee the wind and rain,
> For we shall part so swift again
> As our love came to be."
>
> Then speaks his lover to the lad:
> "Our love shall never end!
> Strong may be steel or iron clad,
> Our love is stronger still:
> Though iron and steel a smith might bend,
> Who can deny our will?
> Though iron and steel in rust descend,
> Our love no pow'r shall kill!"

Our future appeared secure. Scott pulled down a very substantial salary from his lobbying firm. And he waited until his paperwork had cleared and the first of his pension checks had arrived before declaring one Saturday afternoon, "Now I call my parents."

"You want me to stay?"

"Definitely. Pick up on the other phone." He dialed his boyhood Nebraska home. His mother answered. "Mom, is Dad there too? I want to talk with both of you." His father came on the line. "So for the first thing: I've retired from active duty. I've served my twenty years, I'm receiving a good pension, and I have another job."

His father, upset, replied, "When I got you into West Point, I thought you trained as a soldier, not as a quitter."

"Dad, I've seen enough of the service. And frankly, the lobbying group I work for pays much more than I can earn with the Army."

"Weren't 'bout money but 'bout duty."

"Dad, I've made the decision."

"Without consultin' me."

"I'm my own man now," Scott grew angry, "And while we're on the subject, you should know, if you ever call, that I live with another guy. I'm gay and we're in love. I mean to stick with him."

At this point his father began shouting, "You God-damn faggot! 'Own *man*' (he drew out the word) my foot! I raised a fighter not a fairy. Don't you call here again, nancy boy. And if I ever set eyes on that queer piece of shit you live with, I'll shoot him first. just to let you watch him bleed to death. You'll be next, god-dammit!" The phone slammed down.

Scott was sitting on the sofa, and when I came from the bedroom and moved beside him, he slumped back on me, leaning his head on my chest. I stroked his buzz-cut hair and waited quite a long time in silence. He suddenly sat bolt upright and declared vehemently, "I graduated high school at the top of my class. My father just said, 'Well, what you gonna do tomorrow?' And when I graduated fifth in my class at West Point, that miserable old screw commented, 'Shoulda bin first.' When I left Vietnam after two tours, he said that we deserted our allies because guys like me didn't have the guts to fight. I didn't realize until just now how much I've hated him. I'm done. You're the only family I've got now."

"Scott, I'm sorry. Do you think your mother feels the same way?"

"Who knows? She lives in constant terror of that abusive shit. He beat me when I was a kid and he beats her, and that's one reason I applied to West Point in the middle of a war: to get away from him. If there's a just God, one of my father's own harvesters will run him over in the fields and spit him out in shreds. I won't shed a tear." He wasn't dejected but fighting mad, and his jaw was clenched. Adrenaline made him tremble a bit.

"Calm down; how about a drink. And I need to correct you on one point: I'm not the only family you've got. You have my mother and father; I'll bet real money on it. You were brave today, and I need to live up to that tomorrow. You know my folks call every Sunday morning, same time. I want you to get up with me and listen in. Now can I pour you a triple?"

"Let's order some pizza and get totally shitfaced."

"Sounds like a plan to me."

We spent the rest of the evening quietly sousing to kill the pain. And I thought, *well, the worst of that's over.* But that night I awoke in the dark, pinned on my back, with Scott's whole weight on top of me, his hands around my throat. We struggled, and I wondered for a moment whether he was going to kill me. I couldn't scream, but I managed to hit the light switch by the nightstand, and looked up at a face clenched in hatred. As soon as he saw me, he let go, totally surprised, and moved to the side.

When my voice came back I coughed out, "Scott, what the hell?"

"Nick, I'm so sorry." He couldn't face me, but just kept apologizing. Then, "I dreamt I was under attack, ambushed in my sleep." He left the bedroom. When he didn't come back, I went out into our small living room and found him on the sofa, bent over himself. Without moving, he started apologizing again until he finally said, "If you want to call everything off, I'll understand." He was even more frightened than I, if that were possible.

"It's a little late to 'call it off,' don't you think? I've signed on for the whole tour." I added, alarm still in my voice, "It's not like I haven't seen this before. Just not this bad. You need to get some professional help, understand? That's not negotiable."

"I promise."

"Is any of this about your folks?"

"No," he forced out after what seemed an eternity.

"Then what, Scotty?"

"It's a dream about a particular patrol in Vietnam. I can't get rid of it. . . . Could I ask you something?"

"What?"

"Do you ever dream of Chris?"

I was puzzled by the change of subject, "Occasionally—less now than a while ago."

"Do you dream about him dying, I mean when he died."

"No. Fantasies, as if he were still living with me. Sex—really good sex. I can't control what my subconscious pulls up, and to be honest, I don't think I'll ever forget him. Not that I compare you to him, but because I loved him in that special way first and lived with him for two years. Problem?"

"No problem. I understand that. But I haven't been honest with you, Nick."

"How so?"

"I didn't tell you about something—someone—a guy. I meant to do it early on, but Chris had just died, and I kept putting it off."

"A man in Berlin?"

"Fuck you, asshole. I've never been . . . ," he reconsidered, knowing that jealousy was the last thing on my mind. "No, a guy from the war. I . . . just listen." And his secret started to spill out: "I had no idea about preferring men when I was in high school, at West Point. I just didn't have a girlfriend, and I didn't hook up with women like the other cadets on their weekends in the city. On some level I knew guys attracted me, but I thought it came as part of the camaraderie in a male environment, not something erotic.

"Anyhow, after I received my commission in June, 1970 I requested a posting in Vietnam to get some combat experience. When I landed, they immediately assigned me an infantry squad, then a platoon. We pulled duty securing a base perimeter near Hoi An and helping train the South Vietnamese Army. Peace talks had already begun. Everybody knew we would leave the country soon. It all seemed futile.

"I was a second lieutenant when I arrived and more clueless than my enlisted men, certainly less competent than my sergeants. They're the real backbone of any unit, and if you're smart as a new officer, you listen to the NCOs and follow their advice until you figure things out. I wasn't insecure, just inexperienced. They'd offer suggestions, and because they knew the lay of the land and the men, I'd listen and then give commands based on their input.

"There was one especially helpful guy, a staff sergeant in another company. He'd been there for a year already, and at the end of his first tour he signed up for another tour, then a third. When I became a first lieutenant and led a company, he became super friendly even though he wasn't directly under my command. He had smarts, an outgoing personality, and he knew a lot. We established a good rapport, and he helped show me the ropes.

"Now that would've been normal interaction, a bond with a man you fight beside, and I didn't think much about it. But after a year in theater, if you signed up for another tour, you drew R 'n' R in a location out of country. We received about a month for each new tour of duty. I chose Hawaii for my getaway 'cause I'd never seen it. And it looked totally different from anyplace I'd ever been. This sergeant happened to take his second R 'n' R at the same time, and he chose Honolulu too. We were both dressed in civilian clothes, and we happened to meet each another one night in a bar where Army men hung out, shot the breeze. After a night of drinking way too much, we somehow found ourselves back in my hotel room, and he put the moves on me. It felt great—clearly not his first time, though he was only a year older, and he taught me more in bed than he had in theater. We spent ten terrific days together. It caught me completely off guard: I'd fallen in love for the first time, with a man no less.

"Anyhow, between bouts of some totally wild stuff at that swank resort, we talked. And I asked him when he knew he liked to make it with guys. He replied that he'd been stationed in a suburb of Chicago as a teenage corporal tending a radar site. And working a second job, he met what he called this 'beautiful youth,' like a character in some novel he'd read? *The Last of the Wine*?" I felt my chest constrict. "The young man seduced him one night—nothing serious: a little fooling around, really. They hung out for a couple of years until the kid went off to college. Then they met one last time for a weekend in New York—'We never even kissed,' he confessed regretfully. After that visit they went their separate ways. But the sergeant kept recalling the fun they had—and the guy's face and body and voice. He only realized afterwards that he had fallen in love. So instead of continuing at his radar post, he re-upped in the infantry and volunteered for Vietnam. But he still thought of the kid and wondered what had become of him. The sergeant's name . . . "

". . . was Wes Carey," I added in a distant voice.

Scott looked down at the floor, ashamed, "Yeah. Anyhow, we returned to Nam and to those routine patrols, now around Da Nang, securing the port for the remnants of the withdrawing American forces. We were the last Army unit to leave. Having Wes around kept me sane, gave meaning to a senseless time. We spent some weekends in cheap hotels, traded stolen kisses, whatever we could get away with. I thought, well, we'll both finish our tours soon and maybe . . . . I don't know what I imagined would happen after that.

"On one of the last perimeter patrols, a sniper hit Wes, and as he fell, he tripped onto a land mine that blew off both his legs at mid-thigh. I went over to see if I could do anything, and I stepped into a booby trap, one of those pits they dug with sharpened bamboo stakes pointing upward. I ripped my leg open almost to my groin, but I still made it over to him. As he was bleeding out, he tried to say something. And when I pulled his head up to my chest, he murmured 'Nick, Nicky?' Then he was gone. He'd never mentioned your name, and the other men had no clue. After Wes died, I cleaned out his footlocker before sending it back to his family. Out of deference or self-defense, whatever it was, I removed photos of me and him together, and also a snapshot of an intriguingly handsome young man—I assumed the one he had first loved. I dream of Wes over and over, of his face like a fright mask spattered in blood, of his eyes searching and not finding, of his life ebbing away. I can't keep it from coming back, it's so vivid . . . ." He couldn't go on for a while.

Finally Scott regained control of his voice, "Please, Nick, don't hate me, please? When you showed up as a grown man in that Berlin joint, it was like something out of a surreal Hoffmann tale, a figure from a painting come to life. My heart almost stopped when I heard your name. I dug up the old photo to make sure. But at first I didn't want . . ."

"So you knew from the beginning," I interrupted. "Tell me, do you really love me or am I a memento?"

"Jesus!" he muttered to himself. He paused, then answered hesitantly, "What if I answered both?"

I recoiled in shock, thought about it, and replied, "Fair enough. I could have lived without knowing about Wes. But I could never hate you. It doesn't hurt because of anything *you* did, but because I never knew Wes cared all that much. I just thought I had a hopeless crush, and he wanted to experiment. I guess I've walked away from too many men without realizing I'd made a difference. I've probably been shallow and self-centered most of my life. If it's worth anything to you, I'm grateful you were there, and thankful he saw your face last. Was Wes the only man you ever loved? He can't have been the only one you ever . . . ?"

"Actually, yes—the only one I slept with until you. For a long time I felt that if I didn't become involved with anybody again, I wouldn't risk that kind of pain." Scott gazed at the floor, beaten down by the horror of memory and still feeling guilty. Trying to justify what he regarded as his failing he continued, "You've never seen guys die like that. I don't want to relive it. It just comes, unbidden."

"Oh I've seen quite a few men die—just not as suddenly. And I don't want to relive any of that either."

With that Scott collapsed into me. I had never seen him cry. He didn't exactly weep: without any sound the tears streamed down his cheeks. And I held him until he started breathing normally and stopped trembling. Then I poured some liquor into him, drank a few myself, and guided him back to bed.

When the phone rang at 8:30 the next morning, we both had hangovers. But I picked up, shook Scott awake, and motioned toward the receiver in the kitchen, "My parents. I want you to hear."

He moved his lips silently, "I can't do this."

I put my hand over the mouthpiece, "You need to do this for me—and for you."

My mother always came on first in her clipped, German-accented English, "Hello Niki. How are you this morning?"

"A little sleepy. Is Father on the line?"

"No, but I'll call him."

My father picked up, "Hi son."

"I have a favor to ask for the holidays, Christmas really." My parents knew something was up, "I haven't told you, but I've bought this house in Arlington."

"Great son!" My father was happy that I seemed to be settling down, but was still a little puzzled about my line of thought.

"I bought the place with this friend—no, more than a friend, my boyfriend . . . ah, partner."

My mother remained silent, but my father took up the slack, "What's he like?"

"I'll let him tell you."

That put Scott, still groggy, on the spot, "Sir, my name's Scott Willemer, sir."

Nothing went past my father, "Still in the military, Scott?"

"No sir. Just retired."

"As what?"

"Light colonel, sir."

"Then I should address you as 'sir'—I only made it to major. How old, Colonel?"

"42, sir."

"Really? You must have started young."

"West Point, sir."

My father turned his attention back to me, "Nick, what was it you wanted for Christmas?"

"Nothing except for Scott to come back with me over the holidays."

My mother started to object, "I wonder, Nikolaus, if that's a good idea. We're having company for Christmas dinner and then the party on New Year's Day. It may not be the best time to meet this boy."

"Mother, he's a grown man. And if you give yourself half a chance, I bet you'll like him."

At that point Scott broke in, speaking German, "I'd enjoy meeting you, ma'am, and Nick's father."

I could almost hear my mother fall out of the bed where she'd been listening, and I almost dropped the receiver. She came back in German immediately, totally charmed, using the familiar form of address, "Oh, Niki should have told me right away that you spoke German, Scott. You absolutely must stay with us for the holidays!"

My father interjected without further delay, "Then the matter's settled. Book a flight to O'Hare. I'll send a car to pick you up at the airport."

After we all hung up, Scott walked back into our bedroom, "Did I pass muster?"

"Pass muster? I think my mother just adopted you. Want to know why I'm never letting go: you constantly amaze me."

"I hope that lasts a long time." And then he smirked, "So now I know how you came by that Bavarian accent in your German."

"It's an Austrian accent," I corrected. "Remember: Southern Austria–Northern Italy? They share a common border. How long have we known each other, not to mention living together?"

"'How long' doesn't matter: you had me from the first night at the bar in Berlin, with your Italian looks, German eyes, and, okay, 'Austrian accent.' Not to mention all your lip. I'm never letting you go either."

So it came to pass that I found myself in my father's study, Scott and he trading war stories. They spoke of giving orders as officers that endangered their troops (in my father's case, North Italian partisans), about how they came to feel deeply for the men under their command, about the special bond formed during war. Scott observed that at least my father fought for a just cause, and my father replied with quiet directness (for he was by nature an introspective, thoughtful man), "There's no such thing as a 'just war,' because war is always brutally unjust. Perhaps there are necessary wars: World War II arose from self defense. The response in Vietnam was based on the experience in North Korea—we always fight the last conflict. Whether it sent the right message about our resolve to stand against communism only history will tell. Whatever the situation, a soldier answers his country's call, and I can only view that as admirable. Under attack he does everything for the protection of the other men in his unit, not for some abstract cause."

And thus I came to understand, as I listened to their conversation, what attracted me so much to men in uniform: their sense of duty to one another and their bonding. Because my father had experienced that kind of love, he could understand my love for other men, not on an erotic level (which didn't affect him one way or the other), but because the emotional component marked the formative years of his young adulthood.

Eventually the subject of Wes came up, "Whatever happened to that Army boy you chummed around with when you were in high school?" Father inquired. He was surprised that Scott, downcast, answered, "He died in Vietnam, in fact as a sergeant in my division."

"Why do you ask, Father?" I interjected.

"Your mother and I rather suspected that you were more than just buddies. You went everywhere with the fellow, even to New York. I'm sorry to hear he died."

"Why did mother ask later about my being gay, then?"

"By way of confirmation, I suppose. You know it's always been harder for her—her Roman Catholic upbringing, I think." But he wasn't quite finished with the interview, "And that student you lived with, Chris. What happened to him?"

"Passed away from meningitis his third year in graduate school."

"That's a shame, son. You're lucky to have found Scott, then. For one thing, I want to learn his secret for managing my wife."

Scott shot back, "Only if you can give me some tips on dealing with Nick. For one thing, does he ever use normal words? I feel like I'm always attending a college lecture."

"He gets that originally from his mother. When she came to this country, she had to learn English from classes and books. It's like speaking High German all the time, even around the house. Everything had to be 'correct,' and if he used slang, she'd scold, 'Nikolaus: no playground language at home!'"

"Gentlemen, I'm sitting right here." They both continued to ignore me.

My father smiled, "See what I mean: you're out of luck. He's impossible. You'll just need to live with it. And on that note I have one more question."

"Yes sir, what?" Scott seemed to gird himself for an objection.

"Marriage—call it domestic partnership—takes persistent effort. It doesn't always flow smoothly, and sexual attraction, even love, won't sustain a relationship long by themselves. Added to the normal frictions of daily life, you two will have a harder time than most in the outside world. Have you considered the obstacles?" From anybody else this might have sounded like disapproval; from my father it represented sober reflection.

Scott stepped in immediately, "I'm entirely prepared to face whatever comes, sir. And I'm pretty sure that goes for Nick, too." (I readily nodded assent).

They shook hands, and Scott became part of the family. My mother liked him so much that I once quipped, only half in jest, that he was the favorite son. My parents mourned Chris and Wes with us, we had wonderful Christmas and New Year's celebrations, which consoled Scott a great deal. My parents even became accustomed to us sharing a bedroom. "Just like your friends sleeping over when your were a boy, Niki," my mother commented. "No, Adrianna," my father corrected, recognizing the significance of the new ring on my left hand, "not like that at all. Now let them have the room with the double bed."

Plaudite Amici

Family holidays take a toll: constantly up for inspection and on best behavior. When we arrived, exhausted, back at the house in Arlington, we both understood the profound satisfaction of returning to our familiar existence. Thus my cycle of wandering closes the circle, as these opuses sometimes do, with a contented homecoming, the narrator united in somber remembrance and renewed affection with the beloved he had sought. What? You didn't expect a bittersweet ending? You should read the chapter titles before you start the text. Scott, by the way, concludes this tale with his favorite *Lied*:

> Throughout life's sorrow and delight
> We have journeyed hand in hand;
> From wandering we now find respite
> Here above the quiet land.
>
> Vales all around us slope away,
> The atmosphere already fades,
> Just two larks in their climbing sway,
> Night-dreaming, still into the haze.
>
> Step near and leave their flutt'ring play,
> For soon will come the time for sleep,
> Lest we ourselves should go astray
> Within this solitude so deep.

This, then, was our chosen landscape: not one found in a voyage to a distant country but on a journey into the soul of another man—finding sanctuary in its broad still peace.

ABOUT THE AUTHOR

Jon Finson grew up in the northern suburbs of Chicago and attended New Trier High School. He received a baccalaureate degree from the University of Colorado, Boulder, an M.A. from the University of Wisconsin, Madison, and a Ph.D. from the University of Chicago. After a year abroad in Vienna and Berlin supported by The Martha Baird Rockefeller Foundation, he accepted a position at the University of North Carolina, Chapel Hill, where he taught the history of music and American Studies for 35 years.

Finson has published one previous novel, *A Time of Confidences: Novel of Summer* (CreateSpace, 2014), as well as books with Oxford and Harvard University Presses on nineteenth-century German and American music. He holds the 2013 Robert Schumann Prize for outstanding scholarship and editorial work in the promotion of the composer's symphonies and songs. Finson's award-winning edition of Schumann's D-Minor Symphony (1841 version; Breitkopf & Härtel, 2003) is available in the Digital Concert Hall of the Berlin Philharmonic conducted by Simon Rattle.

Made in the USA
San Bernardino, CA
04 August 2017